HIS NAME HAD BEEN

CLEARED OF MURDER.

But there were still people in Ute Crossing who thought that Jim Murdock was guilty. Maybe that's why he had to come back. And maybe that's why he had to find out the truth about the three men who were lynched . . . who weren't as lucky as he'd been that night seven years ago.

Jim Murdock picked up a trail that led him to a ghost town still haunted by echoes of blood and violence and fear . . . a trail that led him to a beautiful, grief-stricken woman who gave him the last clue he needed to rope in the right men . . . a trail that nearly led him to his death.

Because someone back in Ute Crossing had sent out an urgent message to his rough-riding henchmen: Get Jim Murdock. Don't let him talk!

Other Recent Bestselling SIGNET Westerns

BLOOD JUSTICE

by GORDON D. SHIRREFFS

A SIGNET BOOK

Published by **THE NEW AMERICAN LIBRARY**

COPYRIGHT © 1964 BY GORDON D. SHIRREFFS

FOURTH PRINTING

SIGNET TRADEMARK REG. U.S. PAT. OFF. AND FOREIGN COUNTRIES
REGISTERED TRADEMARK——MARCA REGISTRADA
HECHO EN CHICAGO, U.S.A.

SIGNET BOOKS are published by
The New American Library, Inc.,
1301 Avenue of the Americas, New York, New York 10019

FIRST PRINTING, AUGUST, 1964

PRINTED IN THE UNITED STATES OF AMERICA

Chapter One

It was almost time for the first snow of the year. The first cold light of the dawn fingered the dark reaches of the eastern sky, but it was still dark in the valley of the Ute, while the river itself was a dull pewter ribbon against the shadows of the valley floor. The dawn wind had shifted and was driving up the valley, whipping the willows and thrashing the great limbs of the giant cottonwoods of the bottoms. Not a light showed in the sprawling town across the river. It was as though Ute Crossing were as dead as the Indian summer that had just fled to warmer climes. Beyond the sleeping town rose the low approaches to the tumbled, naked foothills, while beyond them, towering over the valley, dominating it while concealing the vast country westward, rose the grim saw-toothed mountains.

Jim Murdock shivered in the searching wind as he rode down the eastward slope of the valley floor toward the bridge that had long spanned the ford that had given the town its name. He hunched the collar of his sheepskin coat up under the brim of his faded stetson, and thrust a cold hand inside the coat to feel for the makings. It had been a long and lonely ride that dark night from the railhead to the east and he should have stayed the night there, but for some reason, unknown even to himself, he had wanted to get back to Ute Crossing as quickly as possible. To some of the people who lived there the name of Jim Murdock was still a bitter thing, almost an epithet, or so he had learned from his brother Ben's long, informative letters. But while there were a few who might remember him with warmer feelings, it was really the country that had brought him back.

He fashioned a quirly, protecting the loose tobacco from the boisterous wind with his broad back, then placed the cigarette between his lips. He snapped a match on a thumbnail and lighted the cigarette, the quick spurt of flame from the match revealing his gray eyes, the mahogany hue of his face, a product of too many border suns, the tiny sun wrinkles at the corners of his eyes, and the thin scar that traced a course from his left cheekbone down to the point of his hard jaw. Looking at Jim Murdock one would instinctively lower his voice and avoid looking for trouble, for here indeed was a lobo of a man.

He drew rein at the edge of the river and looked down at the swirling waters. He eyed the bridge, creaking in the strong liquid grip of the current, and then looked beyond the bridge toward the wide main street of Ute Crossing. It was almost as dark as the inside of a boot. He sat there for a few minutes, drawing in on the cigarette, and when he did so the flare of the burning tobacco made the hard planes of his face almost like a death mask. He would not look up at the gaunt saddle-backed ridge that rose just south of the town and bordered the tumbling waters of the Ute. Something kept him from looking up at that accursed hill that knobbed the near end of the ridge, and yet he knew that if he was made welcome in Ute Crossing and decided to live in that area, he would have to look at that damned hill many, many times in the long years to come.

The eastern sky was faintly lighted by the false dawn when Jim Murdock looked up at the hill, and the sight of the three great trees still standing there struck him like a blow across the face. They, at least, had not changed much in the seven years since he had left the valley of the Ute, saved by the grace of God and a fast buckskin horse. It was almost as though nature had placed those three trees there for some special purpose, for the rest of the hill and the gaunt ridge beyond it were as naked of growth as a suburb of hell itself.

He flipped the butt into the river and slowly rolled another smoke to drive the grinding hunger from his guts. From the looks of Ute Crossing he'd get no breakfast for quite some time. He lighted the fresh smoke and shoved back his hat. Crossing the Ute might be something like crossing the Styx, for there might never be a return. Many people had not forgotten Jim Murdock and his record in Ute Crossing, despite the fact that he had long been cleared of the charges that had sent him pounding through Wind Pass with a posse not too far behind him. There were still hard-eyed men who did not believe that Jim was innocent of the death of Curt Crowley, only son of Big Cass Crowley, the man who had run that part of the country as far back as most people could remember.

He looked up the dark street, and as he did so he saw a quick spurt of yellow light beyond the slab-sided double-decker building that served as the county seat as well as

6

the calabozo. Maybe somebody was opening up early. Someone who could feed a man who had ridden almost thirty miles that night through the windy darkness.

He touched the sorrel with his heels and crossed the bridge to the far side. The horse's hoofs rang clearly on the hard-packed earth of the street. There was another flare-up of yellow light near the building, and for the first time Jim saw what looked like a group of men walking toward the entrance of the jail. He drew rein, narrowing his eyes. A cold feeling of hostility seemed to flow from that group of men, and yet none of them was looking toward the lone horseman near the bridge. They were intent on other business. A thudding noise came from the wide double door.

Jim dismounted and led the tired sorrel into an alleyway beside Slade's Livery Stable. He ground-reined the horse and walked to the dark mouth of the alleyway to look obliquely toward the jail. There wasn't a light on anywhere in the ugly yellow structure. A shift in the wind brought voices to him.

"Get a-goin', Barney," said one man.

"I'm doin' the best I can, Van," said the man at the door. Something snapped and one side of the door opened. "There! Slick as goose grease!"

The men crowded into the building. There were at least fifteen of them, sheepskin- or mackinaw-coated, hats pulled low, hard heels punching into the sagging wooden flooring, spurs chiming softly now and then. Three men stood outside the door, looking up and down the deserted street, Winchesters in hand.

A cold feeling flowed through Jim, turning his blood into what felt like icy red crystals, for there was something altogether too familiar about the scene spread out before him. It was almost as though part of his past were being played out. For an eerie moment the strange thought played through his mind that Ute Crossing was indeed a ghost town, haunted by the ghosts of the men who had broken into the jail one winter morning just before dawn and had hauled Jim Murdock from his cell while there was neither sight nor sound of the sheriff and his deputies.

He could hear them now within the building. A yellow rectangle of light showed where one of the windows was located on the east side of the building, and its bars cast a gridiron shadow on the dirty alleyway that bordered the structure. A cat scurried silently for cover from the revealing light. Something crashed hollowly within the jail, and a man shouted hoarsely. A door slammed.

They were making enough noise to awaken the whole

7

town, thought Jim. But the dark street remained empty, except for the three men who stood outside the jail with rifles in their hands, looking up and down the street and talking in low voices.

There was a clanging of metal against metal within the jail. Once more a man shouted, and then it was very quiet. The light winked out in the cell window.

Jim padded to the mouth of the alleyway. Through the dirty windows of the jail he saw occasional flashes of wavering light, as though a lantern was being carried through the echoing halls. He looked up and down the street. Not another light showed. Not a man moved. The bitter wind picked up dust and gravel and rattled it against windows and walls like a boy playing ticktacktoe on a Halloween night. A tattered newspaper rose from the street, glided upward, and then sailed off to vanish in the windy darkness.

There was a brief struggle at the jail door, and then a man's voice boomed out, "We've got 'em, boys! Jules, you get the horses! Get the three extra ones too, Webb! We can't expect our friends here to ride to the top of the hill!" He laughed loudly.

Jim wet his dry lips. Three men stood among the group. It was easy to spot them in the half-darkness for they did not wear hats. The wind blew the long dark hair of one of them down over his white face.

Two men hurried around the side of the jail and came back with some horses, followed by a third man with more horses. He held a rifle in his free hand.

Jim watched while the three hatless men were hoisted up into the saddles. They could not use their hands for they had been bound behind their backs. The lantern guttered on the jail steps. "Should we take the lantern along, Van?" called out a tall man.

"What for? We don't need any light for this job. Besides, it's almost dawn, Slim."

A boot heel drove against the lantern, smashing it against the side of the doorway, and it winked out. The smell of coal oil drifted across the wide street.

An intolerable crawling feeling came over Jim. Violence and blood were not strangers to him, for a man could hardly be raised in this country, or have spent as much time along the border as Jim had, without being accustomed to it, but there was something utterly alien about the activities across the street, as though these were not men of flesh and blood at all, but rather chimeras conjured up from the depths by some unseen sorcerer who chuckled evilly in the whining

8

voice of the cold, bitter wind that scoured the valley of the Ute. The very evil of their actions and thoughts flowed outward from the group and enveloped Jim Murdock, and for a moment he was almost tempted to turn back, away from Ute Crossing, never to return, for he knew as sure as fate that the evil which had driven him from Ute Crossing was still extant.

There was enough light now to see more clearly. A horse nickered. Another danced sideways as his cursing owner, left foot thrust into stirrup, right hand gripping Winchester, hopped on his right foot trying to make the saddle. "Damn you, Spade!" he said to the skittish horse. "Stand still or we'll miss the hanging!"

What Jim had already realized was now fully proved by the man's statement. These *were* the preliminaries for a lynching; *a hanging at dawn.* The strange thought fled through his mind that such activity might indeed have become the sole occupation of the men of Ute Crossing and its environs. He had left to escape such a lynching, with himself as the victim, and had returned by some Devil's trick, to see another lynching. How many others had happened in his absence? His brother Ben had never written of such activities, but then Ben wouldn't. All he had ever written about was his teaching job, the future of Ute Crossing, the future of its young citizens entrusted to his care to learn to become good citizens. *Good citizens?* By the gods, it seemed to Jim as though lynchers were the only ultimate product of Ute Crossing's citizenry!

Horses were kneed aside to let the cursing man on foot mount his horse. "Stick with him, Lyss!" jeered one of the mounted men. "By God, he'll have his comeuppance when and *if* you straddle him. Hawww!"

There was a sudden movement from one of the bound, hatless men who had been brought from the jail. He raised a leg and slid agilely from the saddle, then ran like a spooked deer across the broad street, his chin outthrust and his eyes wide with fear and panic, expecting at any moment a soft-nosed slug between his shoulder blades. His booted feet slammed against the hard earth. For a moment it looked as though he'd make it from the street, although his chances of ever getting away were impossible.

Two horsemen broke loose from the group. One of them snatched his reata free and fashioned a loop as he rode toward the fleeing man, while the other raised his rifle.

"Christ's sake, Barney, don't shoot!" roared a man from the group. "We want him to swing!"

The fugitive veered, almost as though he expected a loop to drop about his shoulders. He raced toward the alleyway where Jim Murdock stood watching expressionlessly. For a moment he did not see Jim, and then his mouth squared, almost in agony. "For God's sake, mister! Stop them! We haven't done anything! We're innocent, I tell you!" There was a Mexican quality to his voice.

"Trip the bastard up!" yelled the man with the poised loop.

Jim stood aside, pressing back against the worn clapboard of the livery stable. All he had to do was thrust out a foot and the frightened man would drive his face cruelly against the flinty ground, but he could not bring himself to do it.

"Son of a bitch!" yelled the man with the rifle.

The man with the reata reached the alleyway first and threw a neat *peal*, catching the fugitive's feet in a figure-eight loop, as skillful an exhibition of roping as Jim had ever seen. Jim darted forward and dropped to a knee, catching the lassoed man across the chest with his left arm, saving his face from the hard-packed earth. The roper dropped from his saddle and came hand over hand down the rope as though he had roped a calf. "Who the hell are you?" he asked in a brittle voice of Jim.

Jim stood up and saw the man named Barney drop from his horse and plunge forward, stiff-legged, rifle at hip level, lever slamming down and up to load. The metallic sound grated like the creaking of the rusty gates of hell. Jim's .44 was holstered beneath his buttoned sheepskin, and he was twenty feet from his saddle-scabbarded Winchester. The rifleman stopped as Jim rose to his feet. The muzzle of his rifle touched one of the buttons of the sheepskin right over Jim's shrinking navel, and Jim found himself looking into pale gray eyes that were somehow disconcertingly familiar.

The roper coiled his reata and pulled the fugitive to his feet by twisting his free hand down under the man's collar, half choking him. He manhandled him toward the mouth of the alleyway. "Bring that bastard along, Barney," he said over his shoulder.

Jim wet his lips. He stared at the rifleman. "Barney Kessler," he said quietly.

Kessler stared back at Jim. "You know me?" he demanded.

"Ought to. We went to school together at the crossroads," said Jim dryly. "You've come a long way, Barney."

Barney's face looked even more ill-adjusted than it had in the old days. It had always seemed to Jim that Barney was really two different people, each one struggling to get the upper hand and neither ever succeeding, but managing to raise a pocket-sized edition of hell between them in the struggle.

Barney let down the rifle hammer to half cock. "By ginger," he said quietly. "Jim! Jim Murdock!"

Jim smiled thinly. "Now take that gun outa my gut, Barney, like a good boy. This coat is old and too thin to stop a .44/40 at this range."

Barney grounded the rifle. He smiled; then the smile vanished, then reappeared again, while his loose mouth worked a little. "You shouldn't ought to have done that, Jim," he said reproachfully.

"What?" asked Jim.

The smile came and fled. The eyes widened and narrowed. Barney Kessler's face had a way of looking like a picture coming into focus and then as rapidly slipping out of it, so one was never quite sure what he was seeing. "Been in the way," said Barney a little stupidly. The rich, fruity odor of spirits drifted to Jim.

"Come on, Barney!" yelled a man from across the street. "Bring that hombre with you!"

"You got to come along, Jim," said Barney.

"Where?"

"To the hill, of course."

"What for, Barney?" Jim knew well enough why they were going to the hill.

Barney jerked his head. "You're a witness," he said.

"To what?"

"You seen us take them men from the calabozo, didn' you, Jim?"

Jim nodded.

"We don't want no witnesses," repeated Barney.

The picture came clearly to Jim. They'd *invite* him along. He'd be under gun surveillance of course. He'd thus be considered one of the lynchers, unable to bear witness against them. He knew now why the streets of Ute Crossing were so empty, why no early riser's lights were showing.

"Get your hoss," said Barney. "Keep your hands away from that saddle gun."

Jim picked up the reins. He led the sorrel as Barney walked beside him toward the waiting group of men.

"Who is he?" called out a hard-voiced man.

"Jim Murdock," said Barney.

There was a moment's silence, and then a broad-shouldered, meaty-bellied man, kneed his horse toward them. "You're drunker than I thought you was," he said.

"You think I'm bullcrapping you, Lassen?" said Barney in an aggrieved tone. "I went to school with ol' Jim here and we was amigos in the old days, working for Cass Crowley, wasn't we?"

"I hope he didn't come back lookin' for his job with Cass," said another of the men. He laughed shortly. "He sure as hell made a long trip for nothing."

"Shut up, Jules," said Lassen. He peered at Jim. "By God! It's Murdock, all right!"

Jim looked up at the big man. "I see you haven't changed much, Lassen," he said quietly and coldly.

Lassen's eyes, hard as amber, studied Jim. "You always were loose with your lip, Murdock," he said.

"Let's get on with this, Van," said one of the men to Lassen. He looked nervously up and down the street. "We're making enough noise to wake the whole town."

Barney laughed. "Ain't no one going to come out and ask us what we're doing, Webb. You scairt?"

Webb flushed. "One of these days, Barney," he warned.

"You tough, Webb?" sneered Barney. "You wanta make something out of it?"

"Oh, my God," said another man. "The booze is making a fighting man outa Barney again."

Lassen slapped a hard hand down on his thigh. "You men think this is a damned church social? Shut up, I tell you! Maybe Webb is right at that! Look at the dawn!"

The eastern sky was strangely figured in dark and light grays, interwoven with a cold, pearly luminescence.

"Get up on that sorrel, Murdock," said Lassen.

Jim obediently mounted under the cold, hard eyes of the mob. Lassen jerked his head. Jim kneed the sorrel close beside the nearest of the prisoners, the one who had hopelessly tried to escape.

"All right, boys," said Van Lassen. "We all know the way, don't we!"

They clattered toward the eastern end of town where the ridge road ran at right angles to the main stem of Ute Crossing, a tight bunch of horsemen with the three prisoners, and Jim Murdock in the center of the group.

The man who had tried to escape looked at Jim. *"Gracias,"* he said.

12

"Por nada," said Jim politely. He eyed the man. He was Mexican, all right. "You're a long way from home, amigo," he added quietly in his cowpen Spanish.

The dark eyes were sad. "This is a cold country and cold people. I might have expected something like this, amigo. A thousand Jesuses! I am not ready to die!"

"Cut out that spic talk!" snapped Barney Kessler. He slapped a hand on the breech of his rifle.

Jim reached inside his coat for the makings.

"Don't you pull no hideout gun on me!" roared Barney pugnaciously.

Jim withdrew the makings. He looked at Barney. "What kind of red-eye you been drinking, Barney?" he asked mildly. "You're almost talking like a real man."

Lassen laughed dryly.

Jim rolled a cigarette, lighted it, and placed it between the lips of the Mexican. He looked at the other two men. One of them was young, hardly out of his teens, maybe not even twenty yet, and his frightened blue eyes met Jim's with a sick look that almost repelled him. "Smoke?" said Jim.

The kid shook his head. His blond hair fell down over his forehead, and he impatiently threw it back with a toss of his head. The third man was older, plain of appearance, nondescript, looking ahead with no expression on his grizzled face. He looked to Jim like a man who had expected nothing better out of life than to die with a rope around his neck.

"Who's that?" said the man called Webb. He was still nervous.

Jim looked ahead. A slim man stood in the center of the street. His neat black hat was creased fore and aft. His dark coat was set off by a pure white shirt and string tie. His neat boots glistened with polish, and a badge of some sort shone on his coat lapel.

"By God," said Van Lassen. "It's Brady Short!"

Jim leaned forward in his saddle. He had not seen Brady Short for seven long years, and had often thought of him. Brady had been Jim's chief rival for the favor of Ann Whitcomb, only daughter of Judge Enos Whitcomb, chief legal light of that country. Ann had been head and shoulders the best-looking belle in Ute Crossing, if not in the whole valley of the Ute.

"You think he means to stop us, Van?" asked Webb.

Lassen turned in his saddle, and the look on his face seemed to lash Webb across the face like a quirt. "Ain't

13

nobody goin' to stop us, Webb," he said harshly. "Not even Brady Short!"

The riders drew to a halt as Brady Short raised a slim hand.

Chapter Two

"Do you men realize what you are doing?" asked Short.

"We got a pretty good idea," said Barney Kessler brightly.

"Don't give us none of your pretty lawyer talk, Brady," said the man named Lyss.

"I didn't plan to," said the lawyer. He touched the badge on his lapel. "As a deputy sheriff of this county, I advise you to return those men at once to the jail."

Barney guffawed. "Hell's fire, Brady!" he said. "Where'd you get that tin badge? In a box of taffy candy from Gamble's Drugstore?"

The lawyer flushed. "Certainly it's only an honorary title given to me by Sheriff Cullin, and if it doesn't mean anything to you, I then appeal to you as law-abiding citizens not to take the law into your own hands. Take those men back."

"After you've seen who we are?" asked Lassen.

"You didn't expect to get away with it, did you, Van?" asked Short.

"Was you planning to give us away, Mr. Short?" asked Lassen in return.

Lassen's implication was plain enough.

Short swallowed. He was scared, but he stood his ground. "That wasn't my point," he said.

"His point is that he'd make a lot of ground in his chasin' of the judge's position if he managed, single-handed, so to speak, to stop a mob," said a gray-haired man. He shifted in his saddle. "By God, Short, you get to hell outa our way or you'll never get no vote from me, and I been in your party since before you was born!"

Jim studied the lawyer. Brady hadn't lost any of his good looks. He was older than Jim by at least eight years, and the touch of gray at his temples and in his neat moustache had

14

added dignity to the clear freshness the "boy wonder" of the bar in that county had always had, coupled with a sharp, precise legal mind.

"Then you won't listen to me?" said the lawyer.

There was no answer. Hoofs thudded against the ground as though the horses too were anxious to get the business over with.

Lassen jerked his head. The lawyer walked toward his black horse, tethered to a hitching rack in front of the general store. As the group passed he mounted and rode behind them. Jim turned in his saddle. "Hello, Brady," he said.

Brady's dark eyes narrowed. "Jim Murdock!" he said. "What are you doing here?"

Jim shrugged. "Come home to roost," he said with a faint, bitter smile. "Find myself *invited* to this lynching. You follow me?"

Short nodded. "You picked a great time to come home," he said quietly.

"I have a habit of doing such things," said Jim.

"When this is over you must come and see us, Jim. Ann will be glad to see you, I'm sure."

Jim's eyes narrowed. "Ann Whitcomb?"

Brady smiled proudly. "Ann Short," he said. "Mrs. Brady Short, Jim."

Jim felt sick deep within his guts. He had known that Ann must be married by now. He had never asked Ben in his letters about her, for a man's stubborn pride is a hard thing to defeat, particularly in the case of women. It was logical enough she would have married Brady Short. Her father had been the best lawyer in that part of the country. She would have cottoned to one as good as Brady Short. It was in the cards, and the deck had not been stacked.

Jim turned again. He let his horse drift back toward Brady and no one stopped him. Their eyes were on the naked ridge and the ugly hill at the end of it, crowned with its three horrifying trees.

Brady held out a slim hand to meet the hard grasp of Jim's hand. "I did the best I could," he said. "You witnessed that."

"What did they do?" asked Jim.

Brady's eyes narrowed. "You don't know?"

"They never bothered to tell me," said Jim dryly.

"They murdered Cass Crowley," said the lawyer.

Jim stared at him. "Cass Crowley? Old Indestructible?"

"Yes. Cass had been negotiating to sell out his holdings.

15

There was supposed to be a lot of money at his place. Most of his men had been paid off. He was alone at the ranch house. He never had a chance, Jim. Three bullet holes in the back of his head. When Sheriff Cullin caught up with these three each of them had an empty chamber in his gun. Murray Cullin thinks each of them placed a bullet in Cass' head so that each of them would share the guilt. They're sharing the guilt all right."

"Cass Crowley," said Jim in wonderment. "He was like Warrior Peak around here." He looked back toward the saw-toothed mountains. The first light of the dawn was silvering the snow-capped tip of Warrior Peak, the great upthrust finger of stone that had always seemed to admonish the valley of the Ute and the people who lived there. Nothing would ever destroy or bring down Warrior Peak.

The wind was sweeping along the river road, driving dust, papers and tumbleweeds ahead of it into the fence corners and against the trees that bordered the road in between it and the brawling Ute.

Van Lassen turned toward the faintly rutted, almost indistinguishable road that led vaguely up the side of the ridge. It was then that a buckboard was seen in the middle of the road. Its driver was standing up, reins in his left hand, right hand upraised, as Brady Short's hand had been raised back in town.

"It's 'Deacon' Hitchins," said Webb.

The group came to a halt, sitting their horses in the narrow road, hemmed in by the swaying bushes. Van Lassen rode forward. "You aimin' to stop us too, Deacon?" he said.

Jim stood up in his stirrups. It had been seven years since he had seen Alfred Hitchins, local businessman, city father, staunch pillar of the church, a man widely known for his sanctity and honesty, called "Deacon" with respect by one and all, although he had never served in such a capacity. It was Al Hitchins who had helped Ben Murdock get his education after he had been crippled, and who had damned well seen to it that Ben was installed as teacher in Ute Crossing Elementary School; despite the stigma of the name Murdock at that time.

The businessman dropped the reins. "Think of what you are doing, men," he said softly. His round face worked a little. "For the love of the God whom we all cherish and obey, do not do this thing."

Lassen touched the brim of his hat. "We're seeing that justice is done, Mr. Hitchins," he said, not without respect.

"This is not justice, Vanderbilt," said Hitchins quietly.

16

Alfred Hitchins was the only man Ute Crossing knew who could use Van Lassen's first name with impunity.

"You'd better get out of the way, sir," said Lassen.

"I have no way of stopping you. God give me the faith and the strength to do so. Think, men! Think of what you are doing! These men are God's lambs. It is not up to us to destroy them because we believe they have done wrong."

"Some lambs," said Barney Kessler. He looked about, expecting a laugh.

"Shut up, Barney," said Van Lassen shortly.

There was a long pause. The dawn light had almost tipped the eastern range far beyond the valley of the Ute. Slowly Al Hitchins drove his buckboard aside to an opening in the waving brush. The group jingled past up the slope of the hill, and not one of them looked at the man of God; no one except the kid looked at him. His face seemed to plead for help, but there was no help. Hitchins's eyes were moist. He raised a hand. "Jesus wept," he said. No one seemed to hear him except Jim Murdock.

Jim looked up at the three trees. They had a perpetual slant from the cruel battering winds that swept wildly up the valley of the Ute in the late fall, winter, and early spring. Maybe the wind should have felled them long ago, but for some reason they had resisted all efforts of the wind to do so. Battered and gnarled, twisted and ugly, they seemed to reek with an insensate evil. Jim looked away. One of them had almost borne his lifeless body, swinging stiff-legged in the constant wind, tongue protruding, seven long years ago. The sickness returned to his guts and his mind. There was nothing he could do for these three doomed men. Not a single blessed thing!

The horses were reined in. All dismounted except the three prisoners. The Mexican was stony-faced; only his great eyes were alive. The older man bowed his head and stared unseeingly at his saddle horn. Now and then his bottom lip quivered. The kid looked about him with unbelieving eyes. Once he looked quickly down at his trousers, and when he looked up again his face was deeply flushed. No one seemed to notice his embarrassment, but the wind, in its insensitivity to all human feeling, brought the odor of his embarrassment to the hard-faced men who stood there.

The roper stepped out into the open, coiled reata in his hand. He eyed the first of the trees, then smoothly cast the reata, uncoiling like a snake, up over a great limb, while the weight of the loop and honda brought the end down to his feet. Three times he made a perfect cast. He did not look

17

up at the three shivering prisoners as he quickly fashioned a hangman's noose at the end of each of the three reatas.

Barney Kessler swung up on his mare and picked up the first of the loops, widening it quickly, to drop it over the shoulders of the older man. He tightened and placed the knot in professional fashion under the man's left ear. The second loop went about the Mexican's slim neck. The kid bent his head, pressing his chin down against his thin chest to prevent the loop going about his neck. "Come on, kid," said Barney. "We ain't got all day."

The kid turned his head away, pressing down hard on his chin. Barney swung a big hand, catching the kid cruelly over the ear, so hard he must have broken an eardrum. The kid screamed in terror but did not raise his head. Barney drew back his hand once more.

"You hit that kid again, Barney," said Jim coldly, "and I'll break your dirty neck!"

Barney turned quickly. He had left his rifle leaning against one of the trees. There was pure hell in his pale, washed-out eyes. Then his eyes met those of Jim Murdock and his face seemed to slide, dissolve, go in and out of focus.

"He's right," said Webb.

"You keep outa this!" said Barney.

Webb turned a little and moved his rifle. "You heard me, you drunken son of a bitch," he said thinly.

The kid raised his head. "Go on," he said in a choked voice. "I ain't afraid."

Barney saw his out. He wanted no part of Webb and much less of Jim Murdock. "You ain't, kid?" he said in a kindly voice. He smiled benignly, almost like Alfred Hitchins.

"No!" said the kid desperately.

"Then how come you shit your drawers?" demanded Barney. He guffawed. He looked about at the others.

His cruelty struck even hard-faced Van Lassen. "Get on with it, Barney," he said. "Shoulda knowed better than to let you do anything around here."

"Aw, hell, Van," said Barney sheepishly. "I was only joshing."

"This ain't no time for joshing!" snapped Lassen.

But Barney Kessler, no man himself, had effectively stripped the last tatters of manhood from the kid. The boy was completely broken now, a sobbing, retching thing that made even Van Lassen look away.

The Mexican spat to one side. *"Cobarde!"* he said in a low voice to Barney. "Give me a knife, *bazofia,* and we will see the color of your guts! A month's pay they are yellow!"

Barney grinned loosely. "No bets," he said. "This is a serious occasion, spic! Besides, where would you get a month's pay? Shovelin' cinders in hell with the Devil ram-roddin' you?"

Silence came, except for the whining of the wind and the snuffling of some of the horses.

Van Lassen looked up. "You men got anything to say?" he said, not unkindly.

The Mexican shrugged. "One day is as good as the next to die. It is not the thought of dying, hombres, that is painful, only the way of it." He bent his head and mouthed silent prayers.

"You?" said Lassen to the older man.

The man shook his head without raising it.

"Kid?" said Lassen.

"I got a sister," said the kid. His voice broke.

"He's got a sister," jeered Barney.

"Go on, kid," said Van Lassen.

"I got a sister," repeated the kid slowly. "Lives in Three Forks, over the mountains west of here. Name of Jessica. You'll tell her I died?"

Lassen nodded. He looked at Barney. Barney deftly tightened the nooses. Oh, he was good at *that*, thought Jim Murdock. The loose-mouthed polecat couldn't shoot, rope or ride, but he was good at anything like that.

There was a long pause, and then Lassen raised his hand. Three men, one of them Barney, of course, stepped behind the three horses. Barney grinned as he fingered his quirt. Lassen's hand was steady. All eyes were on it. Lassen dropped his hand with a sharp downward stroke. Three quirts struck the rumps of the three horses, and they buckjumped forward in sudden pain and fear. The Mexican's neck snapped cleanly. The older man raised his head, shrieked hoarsely, fought the rope for a moment, and then hung still. The kid fought like a tiger, kicking his legs upward as he fought the killing noose, thrashing and turning, until Barney ran forward and gripped his legs and pulled down on them.

There was a long silence as the three bodies swayed, twisting and turning in the wind, the tree limbs creaking beneath the unaccustomed weight. Although they should have been used to it by now, thought Jim. They had served this purpose before and might do it again. . . .

"Well," said Van Lassen. "There ain't no use in standin' around here freezin' our butts. Come on, boys! We'll drag Baldy outa his sack and get a few rounds of drinks. We earned it, I think."

Jim watched the men mount. Some of them took the riderless horses in tow as they started down the narrow, winding road. No one spoke to him. He was a dead issue now. He had participated in the merciless lynching just as much as most of them had, for he had stood there and had done nothing to save the three doomed men. It was then he noticed that Brady Short had not come up to the hill. Hoofs clattered on the hard earth, leather squeaked, a horse blew. In a few minutes they were all gone, leaving nothing behind but the acrid odor of fresh horse droppings and the cold, almost imperceptible odor of fresh death.

Jim rubbed his bristly jaws and looked up at the three men, and for the first time he realized he did not even know their names, nor had any of the others mentioned their names. The only thing Jim knew was that the kid had a sister named Jessica whom he had wanted to be notified about his death.

Jim slowly rolled a smoke and lighted it, looking up at the three dead men twisting in the wind, swinging stiffly back and forth in the gallows' dance. "Jessica," he said quietly. "How does a man tell a girl named Jessica her kid brother crapped in his drawers just before he was lynched for murder in Ute Crossing?"

There was no answer in the whining wind. It was getting colder and had an edge to its invisible teeth.

Jim felt in his pocket for his clasp knife and then shook his head. No use in him cutting them down, and besides he did not want to touch them, or have any part in their lynching, before or after. Dead men had relatives someplace, who might just come looking for the men who had lynched their kin.

He flipped his cigarette butt away and rolled another. The sun had peeked up above the eastern range, a cold, watery sun that would bring little heat, if any at all, to the valley of the Ute. The growing light had crept across the hills and worked its way down into the valley before Jim mounted his sorrel and rode him down the twisting road toward the river road.

There was a different feeling in the wind. A driving gust of it struck Jim's face like stinging, sharp-edged grit, and it wasn't until he reached the bottom of the slope that he realized that it wasn't grit at all, but the harsh reality of the first snowfall of the year.

Chapter Three

A knot of men sat their horses near the bridge as Jim Murdock rode into the teeth of the wind and the stinging snowflakes. It wasn't until he reached the first building at the southeastern corner of the main street and the river road that he realized the men were what was left of the posse, if one could call it a posse. More like a lynching bee, thought Jim. Some of them were there. Van Lassen, Barney, and the men named Webb, Slim, and Lyss. Brady Short stood to one side, holding the reins of his black, and beyond him Alfred Hitchins sat in his buckboard listening to the words of the tall, broad-shouldered man who sat his gray squarely in front of the hard-faced men who had just hanged three people. Jim recognized the tall man as Sheriff Murray Cullin, one of the best lawmen in the territory.

Cullin held a legal-looking paper in his left hand, the biting wind flapping it about. "I got clear to Benedict Junction late yesterday afternoon," said Cullin, "and sent a wire to the governor for a change of venue for those three men up on that hill there. The wires were down south of town and there was no time to waste. I took the freight train to Parthia and caught a fast passenger run to the capital. Caught the governor ten minutes before he was to leave for Washington and got the change of venue. Took the train back to Parthia, got a fast horse, the fastest horse I could get, and came over Wolf Pass in the dark, pushing that horse all the way, and got here twenty minutes too late! Well, you've had your way, men." He ripped up the paper and let the scraps drift from his big hand. They flew southward with the tiny flakes of snow. "You know what you've done. Brady Short and Mr. Hitchins did their duty as law-abiding citizens to stop you from this crime. You'd listen to no one, would you?"

"You sayin' they weren't guilty, Sheriff Cullin?" asked Slim.

The sheriff's face tightened and he tugged at his dragoon moustache. "Cass Crowley and I were raised together," he said fiercely. "By God, he was like a brother to me! I could have killed those three men when I caught them and no one would have been the wiser, nor would they have cared. But I had the law to uphold. If I break it, then there is no restraint on men like you. The law would have dealt fairly with them, and there is no doubt in my mind that any jury would have found them guilty!"

"Then what's the beef about?" said Van Lassen. "We just saved the county a bill they can't afford right now. Ain't we citizens? Ain't we got rights? Well, we took those rights. We hung 'em, and you can do what you damned well like about it, Sheriff, but let me tell *you* something. You said there wasn't any doubt but what any jury would have found them guilty. Well, you bring us to trial and you won't find any jury that will find us guilty. Not here in Ute Crossing. Not in this county! Not in this whole damned state!"

Cullin shrugged. He knew these men. He also knew Van Lassen was right, and there wasn't anything Cullin could do about it now. He kneed his gray aside and watched the group ride toward the Grape Arbor, not the biggest but certainly the roughest saloon in Ute Crossing, if not in the county, if not in the whole damned state, as Van Lassen had just put it concerning juries.

"An eye for an eye," said Hitchins. " 'Vengeance is mine; I will repay, saith the Lord.' "

Cullin nodded. His eyes caught sight of Jim Murdock. "You," he said coldly.

"I didn't have any choice, Sheriff," said Jim. "They made me go along because I might be a witness against them— as though that mattered."

"I wasn't thinking of that, Murdock," said the lawman.

Jim rolled a cigarette. He looked at the tall man as he wet the edge with his tongue and folded over the paper. "I was cleared of those charges, Cullin," he said quietly.

"Not in my book you weren't, Murdock."

"Are you the sole judge of law around here?"

Cullin leaned forward in his saddle. "I keep two books," he said thinly. "One for those who have not been caught for committing crimes. One for those who have broken the law and gotten away with it."

"And no book for those who have been cleared?"

Cullin smiled without any light in his eyes. "I don't bother with them, mister," he said.

"So you still consider me guilty of killing Curt Crowley?"

There was no answer from the lawman. He turned his horse and rode toward the jail. It was answer enough for

Jim Murdock. He might have expected it from Murray Cullin.

Brady Short led his black toward Jim. "He doesn't mean that," he said.

"Thanks," said Jim dryly. "He sounded convincing enough to me."

Brady studied Jim. "You've changed," he said. "For a moment, when you first spoke to me, I didn't recognize you at all."

"I've been around a bit, Brady," said Jim.

"Where?"

Jim held out the makings to Brady. The lawyer shook his head. "Where, Jim?" he repeated.

"Along the border. Arizona. New Mexico. Texas. Mexico."

"You did all right for yourself?"

Jim smiled. "I worked most of the time," he said. "Made a small strike in the Guadalupes and have an Apache bullet scar on my left thigh to prove it."

"What kind of work, Jim?"

Jim rolled a cigarette. "Stock detective. Texas Rangers for a hitch. Scouted for the Army. You know the usual run of such things. It's been a long time, Brady."

The snow swirled high over the street. Alfred Hitchins had driven silently away, and his buckboard stood in front of the Ute Valley Mercantile Company. He was nowhere in sight.

Jim jerked a thumb over his shoulder, toward the hill and its grisly fruit. "What about them?" he said. "You surely don't want the kids, the future citizens of Ute Crossing, to see these products of justice, do you, Brady?"

"Murray Cullin will take care of it."

Jim drew in on his cigarette. "Who were they, Brady?"

"Drifters. Saddle tramps. Bums. No one really knows who they are or where they came from."

"Figures," said Jim.

"Where are you staying, Jim? With your brother?"

Jim shook his head. "Ben might not like my habits, Brady."

"You are welcome to stay with us. Ann and I have taken over the old Whitcomb place. The old judge passed away last year." The lawyer laughed. "You know how big that place is. We have help, of course. It's quite too much for Ann, you know."

"Any kids, Brady?"

The lawyer flushed. "Well, no. You see . . . I—Well, hang it all, Jim, it's a personal matter really, isn't it?"

"Sure, Brady. Clumsy of me to ask that way."

"You'll come, then?"

23

Jim shook his head. "Thanks just the same. I said Ben might not like my habits. I'm sure Ann and you wouldn't like them either."

"You'll come for dinner, then, sometime?"

"Be delighted," said Jim. He touched his sorrel with his heels and rode a few feet. He reined in and looked back at the lawyer. "The kid has a sister named Jessica," he said. "Lives in Three Forks. West of here, over the mountains."

Brady had a puzzled look on his handsome face. He nodded. He watched Jim ride toward the livery stable, shrugged, then mounted his horse and rode out on the river road, north of town, toward the big house that he called home.

Jim swung down in front of Slade's Livery Stable. Yellow light showed through a dusty, cracked window where Old Man Slade had had his office in the old days. Jim opened the door. An incredibly tall and incredibly thin man, all knobs and angles and no meat, turned quickly from a stove where he was brewing coffee. "Jesus God," he said. "Shut that damned door! We ain't open for business yet, mister."

"Meany Gillis," said Jim. "I thought you had withered away to all bones by now."

Meanwell Gillis eyed Jim with watery green eyes; then he grinned, revealing a gap-toothed mouth. "Jim," he said with genuine pleasure. He thrust out an incredibly thin hand. "Set and have some joe, amigo! Barney Kessler said you was in town."

"He ought to know," said Jim. "Let me put my sorrel up. He needs feed and rest."

"Sure thing, Jim. Lemme open the big door."

Jim went outside as Meany withdrew the bars and opened one of the front doors to let Jim in. Jim led the sorrel into a stall, unsaddled him, rubbed him down, and then gave him feed. He could hear Meany puttering around in the office, and the tantalizing smell of Arbuckle's best brew drifted out to him.

Jim peeled off his coat and hung it on a nail, then walked into the warm office. He twirled a chair and sat down in it, arms resting on the back, chin resting on his arms. "Where's Old Man Slade?" he said.

"Dead five years, Jim. I took over from Mrs. Slade."

"You always wanted this place, eh, Meany?"

The thin one grinned. "It ain't much, but I call it home." He served up the steaming brew in huge granite cups. He sat down in his desk chair and placed the cup on the littered desk. "Seems as though you picked one helluva time to come home, James."

24

"It's a habit of mine, Meany."

The man nodded. "Well, I never believed you was guilty. You can bet your bottom dollar on that, James."

"Why, Meany?" Jim sipped the coffee and felt it begin its good work.

Meany shrugged. "I been around horses all my life. You get to know 'em pretty well, I'd say. Dogs, too. They ain't too different from people, come to think of it."

"How about jackasses?"

Meany grinned. "Meaning you, James? You ain't no jackass, although there ain't nothing stupid about a good jackass. Bullheaded, maybe, but not stupid. Your father was no fool, and Ben certainly ain't."

Jim looked down at the dark circle of steaming coffee. "Seems like I cost my father his ranch supply business. No one wanted to do business with Jim Murdock's father."

"Well, you got to admit Cass Crowley was his best customer," said Meany.

Jim looked up. "And when Crowley stopped doing business with him so did every other rancher in this country."

Meany nodded. "It was like one of them boykits, or something like that, where nobody wants to do business with you."

"Boycott," said Jim. "From what I hear it was more like a quarantine. First it cost me my mother. She wasn't well, and sitting around watching my father worry and get old before her eyes didn't help much."

"Well, like you said, she wasn't well."

"There wasn't anything wrong with my father's health when I left here, Meany."

Meany sipped his coffee. He eyed Jim over the lip of the big cup. "Looks like your troubles cost you your pa and your ma and made a cripple outa your brother Ben."

"Meaning I should have stayed away, eh?"

Meany shook his head. "A man has a right to live his own life the way he wants to, James."

"What about those three men up on the hill, Meany?"

Meany looked away. "Well, what about them?" he echoed.

"Who were they?"

Meany shrugged. "They called them John Does or something like that."

"They had no names?"

"Oh, they gave names all right. No one believed them anyways."

"No one?"

Meany stood up and walked to the dirty window. "They

25

just wouldn't talk. The older hombre was called Gil. The Mex answered to the handle of Orlando. The young one only answered to the name of Kid."

"He has a sister named Jessica," said Jim.

Meany turned. "You know her?"

Jim shook his head. "He spoke about her at the last. He asked Van Lassen to get word to her."

Meany spat into the filthy garboon. "Yeh," he said.

"What do you mean?"

"You ought to know Van better'n that!"

"You mean he won't do it?"

Meany placed a thin hand on Jim's shoulder. "Didn't you know Van was ramroddin' for Cass Crowley when the old man was murdered?"

"There's a helluva lot I don't know," said Jim dryly.

"Cass Crowley was like God to Van Lassen. Maybe more. Ol' Cass was about the only rancher in the valley who could handle Van. By godfrey, he got work outa that man, too! Van seemed to appreciate the fact the old man gave him pretty much of a free rein up at the ranch. If it hadn't been for Crowley, Van would have had to leave this country."

Jim emptied his cup and held it out for Meany to fill it. "What beats me is that Murray Cullin walks outa here and lets those lynchers walk into the jail as sweet as you please. Where was the jailkeeper this morning? Where were Cullin's deputies?"

"They found old Mike Curry, the jailkeeper, out cold in one of the cells with a goose egg on his head. Harlan Meigs was deputy. Well, it seems as though some of the boys got him likkered up in the Ute House Bar last night. He got as far as the jail and passed out in the office. That answer your question?"

"Very neat," murmured Jim.

"Well, they did kill the old man," said Meany. "I don't cotton to lynchings, but they woulda been hung anyways, James."

Jim rolled a cigarette. *"It is not the thought of dying, hombres, that is painful, only the way of it,"* said Jim.

Meany smiled. "Say, that's pretty good! Who said that? One of them Greek philosophers, maybe?"

"Fellow by the name of Orlando," said Jim.

"Was he a philosopher?"

Jim lighted the cigarette and blew a smoke ring. He punched a lean forefinger through the ring. "You could call him that," he said.

The door swung open, letting in a blast of icy air and a

26

swirl of dry snowflakes. A short, potbellied man shook the snow from his hat. "I'll need the team, Meany," he said.

"You want the hearse too, Mr. Dakers?"

"Can't get it up that hill. I'll take the buckboard. I'll need some help. Can you get away?"

Meany shook his head.

"I can't get them down by myself and I can't lift them into the wagon. No one wants to go with me," said Dakers. He shook his head. "I don't know why."

"Maybe the whole town is ashamed of itself," said Jim.

Dakers eyed Jim. "I don't know you," he said.

"Jim Murdock."

Dakers's lips tightened into a straight line. "Oh," he said quietly.

"You've heard of me, then, Mr. Dakers?"

The undertaker nodded. "Some," he admitted.

"More likely a lot," said Jim. He flipped his cigarette into the garboon. "I'll go with you."

Dakers smiled. "That's very nice of you, Mr. Murdock."

"You might get into trouble with the leading citizens by associating with me, Mr. Dakers."

Dakers put on his hat. "My business is with the dead, not with the living. That's my rule, Mr. Murdock. I am a man of rules. I abide by them. Keeps a man disciplined and out of trouble. Follow a good set of rules, I say, and you'll keep out of trouble. Do you agree?"

Jim reached through the door that led into the stable and took his sheepskin from the nail. He shrugged into it and buttoned it. "We'll need something to cover the bodies," he said. "I'll get it." He walked into the stable where Meany was getting the team ready.

Dakers wet his thin lips, helped himself to a cup of coffee, and rubbed his plump jowls. "Jim Murdock," he said thoughtfully. He sipped the coffee. "Business might just pick up at that, after a poor fall season."

Jim led the team out through the front door in a swirling cloud of dry flakes. The wind cut through his thin sheepskin. He swung up into the seat and held out the reins to Dakers. The undertaker shook his head. Jim drove toward the river. There were lights on in some of the stores by this time. A number of horses stood hipshot at the racks, rumps against the biting wind, tails flying every which way. Here and there along the wide street stood men, hats pulled down over their eyebrows, shoulders hunched beneath their thick collars, hands thrust deep into side pockets, watching the

27

buckboard rattling toward the river, and some of the men had eyes for Jim Murdock alone.

Jim halted the team at the crest of the hill and eyed the three stiff bodies swinging like grisly pendulums to and fro, twisting now and then as in some eerie sarabande, accompanied by the wild threnody of the wind and the undertone of the creaking tree limbs.

"Horrible," said Dakers.

Jim dropped to the ground. He took out his clasp knife and walked to the nearest tree.

"Those are fine ropes," said Dakers. "Can't you just untie them? They're worth a few dollars, Mr. Murdock."

Jim turned and looked at the man. Dakers flushed. "Well, there's not much profit in burying such people," he said.

"Did you get paid to bury them?"

Dakers nodded. "Mr. Hitchins stopped in this morning. Gave me a hundred dollars toward their burial. No profit, of course. I might just break even."

"I'll bet," said Jim dryly. He slashed the first rope, then whirled and caught the body of the man named Gil. He carried it to the buckboard and placed it inside. Next he cut down the Mexican and loaded him in beside Gil. For a moment he looked up at the set blue face of the kid, and then he cut him loose and carried him to the vehicle. He severed the taut nooses and threw the foul ropes into the brush.

The wind howled mournfully. It was likely the only sorrow that would be shown for these three unfortunates.

"The digging will be hard," said Dakers. "Business is always better in the early winter, but the ground is hard. Well, we do the best we can in all seasons, eh, Mr. Murdock?"

Jim climbed up into the seat and took the reins. "I wouldn't know," he said. He did not look back as he turned the team and drove down the hill, hearing Dakers's prattle, but not listening to it. Every time the wheels hit a bump or went into a rut he heard something else—the mute, heavy protestations of the bodies in the back.

Jim drove the buckboard up behind Dakers Funeral Parlor and carried the bodies inside for the undertaker, placing them on slabs. Dakers shut the door and took off his hat. "There's no need to hold them," he said. "There will be no one here to see them, poor fellows. Swiftly, swiftly. . . . Ashes to ashes; dust to dust, *et cetera, et cetera*. . . ."

Jim unbuttoned his coat and felt for the makings.

"No smoking in here, Mr. Murdock," said Dakers. "Respect for the dead, you know."

Jim rolled a cigarette and lighted it. He blew a reflective cloud of smoke. "I wonder who they really were," he said, more to himself than to Dakers.

"Their full names are not known."

Jim looked at the man. "Maybe we'd better try to find out," he said.

Dakers shrugged. He felt in his pocket and brought out a limp dollar bill which he extended to Jim. "Here," he said. "For services rendered."

Jim grinned. "Don't put a strain on yourself, Mr. Dakers. Like you said, there's no profit in burying men such as these."

The dollar bill vanished like a gopher into a hole. "If there is anything I can do for you, Mr. Murdock," said Dakers.

"There is."

"Say it, Mr. Murdock."

Jim looked at the bodies. "I'd like to search them."

Dakers frowned. "Why? This is most irregular."

Jim blew a smoke ring. "Someone has to find out who they really were. As far as I can see, no one wants to do that."

Dakers turned his hat around and around in his plump hands. "I can't let you do that. Sheriff Cullin might not like it."

"He doesn't have to know," said Jim.

"I abide by a simple set of rules, Mr. Murdock."

Jim shrugged. He held out a big hand. "I'll take that dollar, then, and two more, one for each body."

Dakers frowned. "Well, it *is* highly irregular, but go ahead." He smiled a rather oily smile. "Any valuables, of course, are to be entrusted to me."

Jim shook his head. "Any valuables go to the next of kin."

"Unknown," said Dakers.

Jim flipped his cigarette into the open front of the stove. "I'll have to ask Brady Short, Alfred Hitchins, or Sheriff Cullin the correct procedure for any valuables or possessions, Mr. Dakers."

Dakers flushed again. "As you please," he said. "Excuse me, Mr. Murdock." He walked into the front of the long building and shut the door behind him, leaving Jim with the dead.

Jim lighted a Rochester lamp that hung over the marble slabs. Swiftly he went through the pockets of the three corpses. He peeled back their clothing and looked for markings of any kind, but outside of manufacturers' labels in some of the cheap clothing there were no identifying marks.

29

Jim drew sheets over the bodies and covered the set blue faces. He heard the front door open and close. Swiftly he gathered up the items he had found and placed them in three different pockets, thus separating them according to the body from which he had removed them. He put out the lamp and left by the back door, coming through the alleyway in time to see Dakers talking to Sheriff Cullin on the front steps of the jail. Cullin nodded and walked with the little undertaker across the street through the swirling snow toward the funeral parlor.

Jim walked past the front of the funeral parlor as the two men walked into the back room where the bodies were. He went quickly to the livery stable and got his cantle roll, emptied his saddlebags of what he required, placed the items in a feed sack, told Meany that if anyone asked for him he'd gone out to see his brother Ben, then hurried through the rear alleyway to the back entrance of the Ute House. He registered for a second-floor corner room overlooking the central part of town and went upstairs.

He closed the door of his room and dropped his gear, then walked to the window, parting the heavy curtains with his forefinger in time to see Sheriff Cullin walk toward the livery stable. Jim grinned. He was unknown to the hotel clerk, so if anyone asked for him and did not ask to see the register, he had time enough to go through the items he had taken from the bodies before Murray Cullin tracked him down.

Chapter Four

Jim peeled off his sheepskin and scaled his hat at a hook. He unbuckled his gun belt and hung it over the back of a chair, then took out the silver-mounted, double-barreled derringer he had won in a poker game in El Paso and checked both chambers. He slid it into a pants pocket. He locked the door and then turned his attention to the three little piles of dead men's relics.

The man named Gil had a left a half-bitten plug of Winesap, a handful of change, a lead pencil with a broken point, a filthy bandanna, and a piece of paper, spotted, wrinkled and limp, with badly written words upon it.

Deer Sarah, [read Jim] I take pencil in hand to write you these few lines. I didn't get the job with Masterson like he said he would but there is a Mex I met at Maddows who is a nice fella, who says he and I can turn a trick or two together north of here. Well I don't know but I am out of scratch and need work so I can send for you my dear Sarah. I hocked my riffle and good saddel in Maddows to a Jew who seems like he is all right for scratch, to go with the Mex who is all right for a spic I tell you Sarah. I can't always have bad luck Sarah and you know no one to home will give me a job because of the old days which are long gone and won't never come back I tell you. I will mail this letter from Ute Crossing which the spic says is a good place for work. Ha ha Sarah any place is a good place of work for me. I say goodbye now and send you my best wishes, and be patent for I will soon have good work and scratch for both of us my dear Sarah.

Gil turned the pitiful letter over. There was no address. Who was Sarah? He shrugged and placed the letter in his wallet, and left the other items on the bed.

Orlando the Mexican had left a little more than Gil. A finely figured Mexican wallet with a badly faded picture of a woman and two little children seated in front of an adobe house with *ristras* of peppers hanging down like great bunches of fruit. He turned the picture over. He could just make out the faded words "Santa Fed . . ." There were a few Mexican bills in the wallet. A tobacco pouch and a few sweet Mexican cigarettes. A gilt button with the Mexican coat of arms of snake and eagle and the letter C embossed below them, likely from an army uniform. There was a worn leather box about the size of a medal box. Jim opened it. A beautiful, though worn, hunting-case watch was set in the faded green velvet. He opened the lid and looked at the dial. "American Horologe Company, Waltham, Mass.," he read. He worked a thumbnail under the back cover and snapped it open. A fine script had been engraved within. "To Teniente Teodoro . . . . For heroic services rendered at Colonia . . . ." read Jim. Part of the lettering had been scored through, making the names impossible to read. Jim closed the back cover and wound the watch. He pressed the repeater button and heard the expensive timepiece strike the nearest quarter hour. A helluva fine watch for a saddle bum to be carrying, but then it was likely stolen. The only other item left was a *barbiquejo* hat strap with coin-silver ornamentation.

The kid had left practically nothing. An empty bag of Ridgewood cigarette tobacco with a curious-looking bluish stone in it. A worn handkerchief. A box of matches, Round Dome Specials, with two matches still in it. A 'dobe dollar. A hardened half bar of Pears' soap. That was it, and the name of a sister—Jessica. . . .

Jim swiftly made his choices. He took the Mexican's picture, the gilt button, and the expensive watch. From the kid's possessions he took the curious-looking stone and nothing else. He could easily remember Round Dome Special matches and Pears' soap. The soap was common enough in that country; the type of matches was not.

Hard knuckles rapped on the door. "Murdock?" said a familiar voice. It was that of Murray Cullin. Jim walked softly to the garboon and placed the button and the watch in it. He slid the picture under the edge of the marble-topped dresser and the stone under the edge of the rug.

"Murdock? You in there?"

Jim picked up the lint-specked wad of Winesap and bit off a chew. He peeled off his vest and shirt and threw them on the bed, then walked to the door and opened it.

Cullin brushed past Jim and looked about. He saw the items on the bed. "What's this?" he said.

"Must be what you're looking for," said Jim. He worked his chew into pliability.

Cullin poked through the things with a spatulate finger. "You had no business taking these things," he said.

"Why? No one around here seemed interested in who those men were."

Cullin looked around the room, glancing at the worn walnut butt of the holstered Colt. "No one knew who they were," he said. "They wouldn't give their real names."

"John Does to you, eh, Cullin?"

Cullin turned slowly and studied Jim. "What's your game, Murdock?" he said coldly.

Jim leaned against the wall and shrugged. "Someone should notify the next of kin."

"Three killers? Is it worth it?"

"Cain had relatives," said Jim. "They must have been interested even in him."

"You've got a great sense of humor, Murdock. Maybe you've even read a book in your time."

"Some," admitted Jim.

Cullin poked through the items again. "Like your brother, eh?" he said.

"Maybe even you could learn something from him, Cullin."

Cullin turned again. "Put up your hands," he said.

Jim straightened up. As he did so he spat a juicy gob into the garboon. Cullin's practiced hands felt about Jim's hard body. "I didn't know you cared," murmured Jim.

Cullin took the derringer from Jim's pocket. "You could get into trouble with one of these stingy guns around here," said the lawman.

"Is there a local ordinance against it?"

"No." Cullin dropped it into Jim's pocket. He looked about the room again.

Jim walked over to the garboon and spat into it again.

"Filthy habit," said Cullin.

Jim wiped his mouth. "I wasn't brought up right," he said.

"That's a damned lie," said Cullin. "You came from fine stock, Murdock."

"As the twig is bent," said Jim.

Cullin looked about the room again. "What are your plans?" he said.

"Get a bath. Change these clothes. Get some breakfast."

"Damn it, Murdock! You know what I mean!"

Jim shifted his chew. "I don't know, and if I did know, I'd be damned if I'd tell you, Cullin."

The sheriff looked down at his big hands. "Sometimes it pains me to uphold the law. There are times when I'd enjoy breaking it myself."

"Any time. Any time," murmured Jim politely.

"You never avoid trouble, do you?"

Jim leaned against the wall again. "I didn't exactly want to go with those human wolves this morning, if that's what you mean."

"That's not what I meant."

Jim shrugged. "If you mean my coming back to Ute Crossing, then I say to you that I was cleared years ago of the charge of killing Curt Crowley. It went as high as the governor and he OK'd it, Cullin. Even in the face of Cass Crowley."

Cullin's eyes narrowed. "Just what do you mean by that?"

"You know as well as I do that the governor was just as afraid of Crowley's political power in this state as most officials are."

"Does that include me?"

"You've been sheriff for a long time, Cullin."

Cullin ground a balled fist into the palm of his other

33

hand. He walked to the bed and picked up the items there, dropping them indiscriminately into the side pockets of his coat.

"How will you know who owned those things?" said Jim. "In case anyone happens to ask for them."

Cullin walked to the door and turned. "I want no trouble from you in this county, Murdock. I have nothing but the greatest respect for Ben, like most people around Ute Crossing do, and I really believe Ben thinks he cleared you, but in my book you were never cleared. You walk quietly, mister. You walk *very* quietly." He opened the door and walked out.

Jim spat viciously into the garboon without thinking. He locked the door and then retrieved the watch and button. He wiped them off and pocketed them.

The snow was still falling when he finished his bath and dressed in fresh clothing. He placed his hat on his head and eyed himself in the gold-flecked, tarnished mirror. "You handsome dog, you," he said with a grin. "By God, you just walk quietly, mister, you just walk *very* quietly."

He ate well in the busy restaurant next door to the hotel, and was acutely conscious of the surreptitious glances he got from some of the other patrons. He bought half a dozen short sixes and stowed them away in his cigar case, lighting one of them at the counter before he strolled out into the open air and stood watching the falling snow beyond the wooden awning. The wide street was already an inch or more deep in snow, scored by hoof and wheel tracks. He'd have to go out and see Ben. He had mixed feelings about seeing Ben again. Ben had developed a penchant for preaching in his last letters, and Jim wasn't quite in the mood for sermonizing. "Settle down," Ben would say. "Get a nice wife. Get a steady job. Raise a family. Teach your kids the difference between right and wrong. Respect for the law."

Jim looked in the direction of the gallows hill. Nature was trying its best to hide the sight from the eyes of the people of Ute Crossing, but it could never erase the thought of what had been done there that very morning from the minds of every man, woman, and child in Ute Crossing. The ugly story would spread throughout the valley of the Ute and over the mountains with incredible speed, and the whole state would know about it before the start of the next week. This was Saturday morning. By Friday the story would have spread throughout all the neighboring states, with variations, embellishments, and changes to suit the taste and imagination of the teller.

He'd have to see Ben. Jim walked to the stable and got

a fresh horse from Meany. Ben lived three miles from town in a little place he had bought after he had sold the old Murdock place south of town. There had been too many memories, he had written, and being a cripple, he could no longer handle the place. All his life now was devoted to teaching. He'd be a good teacher, thought Jim, as he guided the gray from the stable and rode west along the main stem, sheepskin collar turned up high, cigar thrust out from taut jaw, eyes far away from Ute Crossing. For some odd reason he was thinking of a girl called Jessica.

If Jim Murdock's mind was far away as he rode out of Ute Crossing that morning, there were others that were quite conscious of his physical presence in the town. Four pairs of eyes peered through the dirty, streaked windows of Baldy Victor's Grape Arbor Saloon.

"I didn' like the way he talked to me this morning," said Barney Kessler. He hiccupped. "Him and me was amigos in the old days, all through school. I rode fence with him for Cass Crowley, too. Taught him all I know. Ridin', shootin', brandin' and roping. You seen the way he acted toward me."

Buck Grant, the man who had roped the Mexican Orlando and who had strung up the reatas to lynch the three prisoners, looked sideways at Barney. "*You* taught *him* ropin', Barney." He grinned loosely. "That's the best one I heard today."

Lyss Adams wiped his mouth and shifted his chew. "What'd Murdock have to show up today for, anyways? It was almost as though someone tipped him off to what was goin' to happen."

"You talk like a man with a hole in his head," said Baldy Victor as he wiped the bar. "Ain't no reason Jim Murdock would want to come back to witness a lynching. He come so goddamned close to one himself he wouldn't like to see another. He likely come back to see his brother."

Buck Grant turned from the window. "Yeh, but why, Baldy? Ben Murdock's been doin' a lot of talkin' around here. Drives like a madman into town in that buggy of his, lowers his wheelchair to the ground, then rolls that damned thing all over town. He wants to talk to them prisoners. He gets Murray Cullin all riled up. He sends a telegram to the governor. He tells the kids in his school them three hombres we strung up are innocent until proven guilty. That's the best I heard yet."

Van Lassen leaned his meaty belly against the bar and

curled a huge hand about his glass. "He was right about that, anyways."

"You mean we done wrong?" challenged Barney. "It was you who got the idea, Lassen."

"Shut up!" said Lassen. "I get tired of hearing you run off at the mouth."

They all lined the bar. Lyss shifted his chew and spat into the garboon. It rang with the wet impact. "All the same, what'd Murdock come back today for?" He looked at Lassen. "By God! You don't suppose he's a lawman, do you, Lass?"

Lassen's flat amber eyes studied Lyss. "So what if he is?"

"Well, we ain't got Cass Crowley around no more. Sure, we avenged him, like it says in the Bible, but he's gone now. Supposing Murdock is representating someone away up."

"Like God, maybe?" jeered Barney.

Lyss shook his head. "Like the governor, maybe?"

Buck Grant laughed. "The governor does what he's told in this state. He don't make no decisions."

Lassen looked down into his glass and then drained it. "There's another government, you know," he said quietly. "The federal Government." He did not look at the others.

It was very quiet in the saloon. Boot heels struck the wooden sidewalk outside. A dog barked. Baldy passed a moist hand over his shining skull.

"That's a lotta crap," said Barney boldly. "Ain't no jury in this state would prove us guilty, like I said this morning."

"*You* said this morning," mimicked Grant.

Lassen looked into the mirror behind the bar. "I don't like this," he said slowly. "Ben Murdock is a pain in the rump, always shootin' off his mouth about rights, justice, good citizenship, and all that crap, but Jim Murdock is a fightin' man. He always was and he always will be."

"Until someone cuts him down," said Barney loudly.

It was very quiet again. They all looked at each other.

Baldy Victor rubbed his jaw. "The drinks are on me," he said. He did not look at the four men as he said it.

Jim crossed the creaking bridge that spanned Warrior Creek. The swirling water was black against the newly fallen snow. To the south was the old Murdock place on the banks of Warrior Creek. The sight of the creek brought back many old memories to Jim. Ranching had been in his blood in those days, and until he had gotten into trouble for supposedly shooting Curt Crowley, he had practically run the Murdock ranch alone, for Ben, when he wasn't talking, always had his nose in a book and his thoughts on going to college. Well, he had finally achieved his hopes for an education—the hard way. Substituting a schoolroom for the open range and wheels for legs.

The low bridge rails were capped with snow, and the flooring of the bridge was untouched as yet by wheel or hoof tracks. The black water looked icy cold to Jim, almost as though it would freeze solid at any time.

A wraith of smoke curled up from Ben's chimney and vanished in the snow. There were no other houses anywhere near the place, which likely suited Ben fine, for he wasn't much for company except in the schoolroom, or with men like Brady Short and Alfred Hitchins, who could match Ben's intellect and his thirst for knowledge.

Jim swung down from the gray and led him into the little barn where Ben kept his team. Jim eyed the two sleek mares Ben used to pull his buggy. He wondered if Ben still drove like Jehu. Ordinarily quiet and introspective, not given to sudden words or sudden movements, Ben seemed to change when he gripped the reins. One mare would have been aplenty to pull Ben's buggy, but Ben liked two. That team must have set him back a good piece of change, particularly on a schoolteacher's salary.

Jim walked around to the front of the house and rapped on the door.

"Who is it?" a familiar voice called out.

"It's Jim, Ben."

There was a moment's pause, and then a chain rattled behind the door and a key turned in the lock. The door swung open and Jim saw Ben seated in his wheelchair. For a moment Jim stared. Ben was only five years older than Jim, hardly thirty-three as yet, but he seemed to have aged immensely in the seven years since Jim had seen him. His hair was almost pure gray and his face was deeply lined. He held out a thin hand to Jim and gripped it tightly. "Why didn't you tell me you were coming home, Jim?" he said quietly.

"I wasn't sure I was coming, Ben."

Ben closed the door. He reached for the key in the lock, glanced uncertainly at Jim, then wheeled himself over beside the marble-topped table. A book lay open in the yellow light from an Argand lamp. "You might have let me know, Jim," said Ben.

Jim peeled off his coat and hung it and his hat on a hall tree. Ben's eyes flicked down to Jim's waist and saw the familiar bulge of holstered Colt beneath the dark coat. He narrowed his eyes.

Jim sat down and held out his cigar case to Ben. Ben shook his head. He watched Jim light up. "It didn't take you long to get into the swing of things," he said.

Jim looked through the wreathing smoke. "You heard about the lynching? I hardly had a choice, Ben."

Ben waved a hand. "I know that. You just seem to have the Devil's own luck."

Jim shrugged. "Seems as though no one will be called to account for it. Van Lassen practically defied Sheriff Cullin to do anything about it. Lassen said no jury in the state would convict them."

Ben drummed thin fingers on the table. "He's right," he said quietly. "Cass Crowley is here in death as he was here in life."

Jim inspected the end of his cigar. "There are no Crowleys left," he said.

"Cass Crowley had a host of friends," said Ben. "He was a hard man in many ways, but an honest man."

"Except in politics," said Jim.

Ben nodded. "That seemed to be an obsession with him. I never quite knew why. He had everything. Money, respect, position, and everything else most people want."

Jim leaned back in the chair. "Well, maybe Van Lassen was right when he said he'd save the taxpayers some money." He studied Ben as he spoke.

Ben flushed. "You talk like a fool!" he said hotly. "This is not justice! For hundreds of years we've struggled to have justice. Laws that punish and protect. Guilty or not, those three men had a right to the due process of law."

"To get hanged anyway," said Jim dryly.

"You've lost the point," said Ben coldly. He looked closely at Jim. "The very reason I fought to clear you is why I was fighting to help those three men, Jim. I was afraid something like this would happen. I *knew* it would happen!"

Jim relighted his cigar. "Why, Ben?"

Ben looked back at the door and then at the windows. "The evidence that was brought against those men did not satisfy me."

"It seemed to satisfy Brady Short, Alfred Hitchins, and Sheriff Cullin. Not to mention Meany Gillis and Mr. Dakers, the undertaker."

Ben leaned forward. "It was circumstantial evidence that was brought against you, Jim. Supposing I had not believed you were innocent?"

"I wouldn't be here now."

"Exactly."

"Then you think those men were innocent?"

"I do not."

"Then what's bothering you outside of the fact that the law was broken this morning?"

Ben looked again at the door.

"You want me to lock it again, Ben?" said Jim.

Ben quickly turned his head, and there was a faint trace of fear in his eyes. "No," he said.

"What's bothering you, Ben?"

Ben closed his eyes. "Make some coffee," he said.

Jim studied his brother. "You've been making trouble for yourself," he said. "You ought to know better than to stick your nose into every law case in this county. You've got no right to do that, Ben."

Ben opened his eyes. "It is the right of every good citizen."

"You're not in the classroom now, Ben."

Ben slammed his fists down on the arms of his chair. "You talk like a blind fool!" he said. "Go make that coffee before I lose my temper!"

Jim stood up and shrugged. The glass of the window just beyond his chair was suddenly shattered. Something smashed into the Argand lamp and hurled it from the table against the wall, splattering kerosene against the carpeting and the wallpaper. Ben grunted in savage pain as glass splinters lanced into his cheek. The report of a heavy rifle came echoing from somewhere across the creek.

Jim shoved his brother's wheelchair into a corner and dragged him from it. "Stay down!" he yelled. He dropped flat and bellied toward a window. The window shattered just over his head, and he winced as broken glass tinkled on the floor and struck his back and the back of his head.

Flames licked along the edge of the carpet and danced on the wooden floor, while a tiny runnel of flame worked its way along the soaked wallpaper. Jim snatched up a rug and beat out the flames. A cold wind poured into the room from the two shattered windows.

"Where's your rifle?" demanded Jim.

"I don't keep any guns," said Ben.

"That figures," said Jim dryly.

Minutes ticked past. There was no sound except the icy rushing of the snow-laden wind around the little house.

Chapter Five

Jim finished hanging rugs over the two shattered windows, nailing them to the frames, and then he walked warily outside to close the shutters. There was no sign of life in the shallow valley of the Warrior. The snow had lightened but there was still quite a bit of it, and the wind was much colder. Jim walked back inside the house and leaned his Winchester against the wall. Ben had lighted another lamp and was in the tiny kitchen making coffee. Jim dug the two slugs out of the wall. They were .44/40s, about as common a caliber as one could find in that part of the country, and throughout the West, for that matter, as they were interchangeable between rifle and pistol.

Ben rolled his chair back into the living room and placed the coffeepot on the table. "Cups in that cabinet there," he said. His face was white and taut.

Jim got the cups. "Why, Ben?" he asked.

Ben looked up. "They were after you," he said.

Jim filled the cups. "Why the double lock on the door?" he asked. "Why the look of fear in your eyes? You can't fool me, Ben. Who's been hurrahing you, and why?"

Ben measured sugar and cream into his cup. "I don't really know," he said. He looked up at Jim. "It was like the beating I got when I was fighting to clear you. I've never found out who did it."

"When did this start?"

"About the time I got interested in those three prisoners."

Jim sipped his coffee. "Seems odd," he said. "They were certainly guilty from what I've managed to learn. Were there any other suspects?"

"None."

"Maybe you should have kept your nose out of it, Ben." Jim smiled and raised a hand. "I know. Justice!"

"You're getting the idea," said Ben dryly. "I still say those shots were meant for you."

"He was a lousy shot, then," said Jim.

40

"Across the creek with the snow coming down? I think he did very well."

"That's because you're no rifleman, Ben. The range was hardly more than seventy-five yards, with the wind behind him and me silhouetted between the lamp and the window. I will admit I stood up just at the right time."

"All right, then! What do you think it was? Was it me or was it you they were after?"

Jim lighted a fresh cigar. "It was a warning for me," he said. He looked over the flame of the match. "You can bet your bottom dollar on that."

"What makes you so sure?"

Jim shrugged. "I didn't make myself too popular this morning. Besides, there's something else I intend to do."

"Such as?"

Jim took out the items he had taken from the bodies of the three lynched men. "Someone has to tell their people they died."

"That's not up to you."

"No one else seems much interested."

"They were tramps, Jim. Nobodies. Drifters. They saw a chance to kill Cass Crowley and they took it. They knew they'd never get away with just robbing Cass Crowley. They *had* to kill him."

Jim smiled. "Who's making up evidence now, Ben?"

Ben flushed. "All right! All right! It just doesn't make sense, your going away like this. How can you find their people, anyway? No one ever found out their real names or where they came from."

Jim eyed the little pile of possessions. "I'll try," he said.

"It might take a long time, and what profit is in it for you, Jim?"

"I've got the time," said Jim quietly. He looked at his brother. "It's my way of doing things, Ben. You've got your teaching and your interest in justice and citizenship. You cleared me, but it was me who damned near ended up on that hill with a rope around my neck in the cold light of dawn. It was me who stood up there this morning and saw those three wretches get strung up like pigs to be slaughtered."

Ben narrowed his eyes. "Go on," he said softly.

Jim looked at his brother. "The kid had a sister named Jessica," he said.

"So?"

"Someone has to tell her, Ben."

"I had hoped you'd stay here with me for awhile. Settle down. Get a nice wife. Get a steady job. Raise a family.

41

Teach your kids the difference between right and wrong. Respect for the law."

"Oh, God," murmured Jim. I knew it, he thought. I just knew it!

Ben's jaw tightened. "I've had my say," he said.

Jim stood up and drained his cup. "I've got a room at the Ute House," he said.

"I thought you'd stay with me, Jim," said Ben in a hurt tone.

"Later, Ben. I've got some plans."

"Sure! Sure! Gambling! Booze! Women! Is that it?"

Jim couldn't help it. "What else is there?" he said. He looked about the room. "I'll leave my rifle here and pick up a gun in town for you."

"I don't need any."

Jim shrugged. "As you will." He looked down at Ben. "These three men who were lynched. Tell me all you know about them, Ben."

Ben emptied his cup and refilled it. "They came from the south, maybe from New Mexico, about a month ago. One of them was a Mexican. They camped over on the Blue for a spell. Cullin later found traces of their camp there, and a sheepherder said they bought coffee from him. They told him they would be looking for jobs around Ute Crossing. Van Lassen was still working for Crowley then. It was him that found Crowley in his living room with three .44 slugs in the back of his head. The place had been ransacked. Lassen notified Cullin. Cullin formed three posses. One headed over Wind Pass. One headed west toward the Warrior Peak country. Cullin himself went back to the ranch with the third posse. It was Cullin alone who found the three killers hiding out near Brushy Creek. Cullin himself rounded them up. Murray Cullin has more solid guts than a brass monkey."

"So they were brought in to Ute Crossing."

Ben nodded. "There was a lot of talk going on in the saloons. Some of Crowley's riders and friends were ready to hang the three of them right then, but Murray Cullin isn't the man to be bluffed, and you can thank God for that. Brady Short suggested a change of venue, for everyone was clamoring for a trial, and you know what would have happened if a trial was held in this county."

"I have a good idea."

"One of my pupils heard the shooting over on the creek when Murray rounded up the three of them. It didn't last very long. They didn't seem to be desperate men to me."

Jim nodded. He could see the three of them as though

they now stood in front of him. "That's the whole story, then?"

Ben nodded. "Cullin kept a close guard over them. I suppose he was afraid of what would happen if he relaxed."

"Harlan Meigs sure relaxed last night," said Jim dryly. "The boys got him drunk as a hoot owl in the Ute House Bar last night. He was out cold in the office when the mob broke in. Old Mike Curry was laid out cold too. Maybe never had a chance to wake up."

Jim shrugged into his coat and put on his hat. "You sure you don't want a gun?"

Ben looked up. "That shot was for you, Jim. It was a warning. Why, I don't know."

"Maybe a lot of people still think I killed Curt Crowley." Ben nodded.

"The only way they'll ever believe I'm innocent is when they find Curt's killer." Jim placed a hand on Ben's shoulder. "I'll be all right in time, Ben. Let me do what I want to do. Maybe then I'll come live with you and try to make something out of myself. After seven years I can't place myself in harness. Give me a little time, eh, Ben?"

Ben looked away. "You haven't changed much in some ways. You left here a wild, gun-flashing hellion. You don't seem wild now, and I don't know anything about your gunplay, but there is still much of the lobo in you. I had hoped for something better, Jim."

"The Mex border isn't exactly the place for peaceful pursuits, Ben. Besides, you've got a profession. You're a respected teacher. Me, I live the only way I know how. You talk about the law and justice, but all you really do is talk. No offense to you, Ben. There are some of us who have to do the dirty work, and being a lawman is accepting that kind of work. Murray Cullin will tell you the same thing."

"He still thinks you killed Curt Crowley."

"You proved I was miles away when Curt was killed."

"I proved that to the governor. I never convinced Cullin, or a lot of other people, for that matter. Curt Crowley was popular, Jim, and he was the son of Cass Crowley. Likely if it had been anyone else around here you would have been forgiven. Then, too, you were a hellion, as I said before." Ben looked up at his younger brother. "You know, kid," he added quietly, "if I could walk and ride again, I think I'd do the same thing you are doing."

"Change of heart?"

Ben shook his head. "There is a streak within us Murdocks that calls for justice, for doing things right. I don't know whether or not you will find the people of those three men, but in the search you will learn something. Something that you will never learn here."

"I'll see you before I go, Ben."

"I hope so, Jim."

They shook hands. Jim closed the door behind him and shivered in the biting wind. The snow had stopped and the sky was a steely gray, and the cold was a living thing.

He rode slowly back into town, cigar clenched in his even white teeth, his thoughts were miles away at times, but his eyes shifted constantly, studying each snow-covered mound, clump of trees, hump of rock, any place that just might afford enough cover for a rifleman. He knew that shooting had been a warning. Someone either wanted him to forget about finding the relatives of those three dead men, or wanted him to mind his own business if he stayed in Ute Crossing. He ran quickly through his mental file. He had hardly made any new friends, or renewed old acquaintances, since he had returned to Ute Crossing.

He spent several hours in making purchases for his search and knew, without doubt, that his activities had been observed. He placed his supplies in the livery stable and went back to his room. He wasn't in the room two minutes when he knew someone had been there in his absence. The room was as neat as when he had left, but someone had been up there.

Jim stood for a long time at the window, watching the slow approach of the winter dusk. At last he lighted the lamp and took out the cheap atlas he had bought in the general store. "Maddows," he said thoughtfully. He scanned the listing of towns in this state, as well as those that bordered it to the south, finding no such place as Maddows. The man named Gil had mentioned such a place. All Jim really knew was that Gil had been at such a place and that it was south of Ute Crossing. He located the Blue, a creek high in the rough mountains southwest of Ute Crossing. The three men had camped there for a month and had said they were moving north to Ute Crossing. Jim scanned the country in the area of the Blue, but there was no Maddows. The best he could do was to start southwest to the country of the Blue and work from there. Somehow he did not want to find Three Forks and the girl named Jessica until he had first found out about the man named Gil. He had almost canceled out the Mexican. He had no great desire to return to the border country at this time.

Someone rapped on the door. It was the lone bellhop of

44

the Ute House, with a message from Brady Short. It was imperative that Jim come and see him as quickly as possible. Jim put on hat and coat, put out the lamp, and hurried to the stable to get the gray. The wind had stopped and an icy hardness was settling over the country, unusually cold weather for that time of the year. The gray's hoofs rang on the iron-hard road as Jim rode north to where Judge Whitcomb had built his great house so many years past.

He saw the lights of the house long before he saw the house itself. Ann would be there. She had been nineteen when Jim had left Ute Crossing. An ash blonde with hazel eyes that could cut a man's heart to pieces like a Mexican *saca tripas*. It had almost been a foregone conclusion that Ann would marry Jim. The old judge hadn't been too happy about the matter. It wasn't Jim's family he had been concerned about. The Murdock name stood well in that country, and the judge had served with Sam Murdock in the volunteers during the war, down New Mexico way, and Sam Murdock had saved the judge's life at Glorieta. No, it had not been the family. Elizabeth Murdock had been a Hobbs, descendant of one of the pioneer fathers of the state. Ben had always ranked well among the young people of Ute Crossing. It had been Jim who had caused Jonas Whitcomb concern.

Now the Murdock family meant little. Elizabeth, never very strong, had died, and Sam Murdock had failed in his business and had passed on to his reward. Ben Murdock, a cripple, was still held in respect by Ute Crossing, but Jim had not gilded his own laurel wreath, if he had ever rated one. Sure, he was a fast gun, a good man with rope and branding iron, but the stigma of the brutal murder of Curt Crowley still hung about him like the dead albatross carried by the Ancient Mariner, no matter that Ben Murdock had cleared Jim's name.

He reined in the gray at the white picket fence and looked up at the familiar house with the wooden turrets, the gingerbread, the many tall windows with colored glass at the top, the wide verandas thick with crusted snow, and the swing swaying idly in the cold cat's paws of wind that crept now and then down the valley of the Ute. Jim remembered that swing. He wondered idly if it was the same one.

He led the gray into the huge barn and into a stall. There were at least a dozen other horses in the stalls. Brady Short had never been much of a rider, but he liked matched teams for his buggy, surrey, or buckboard. Jim wondered if Ann still rode as she had in the old days. The two of them had covered every mile of the valley of the Ute. Something

45

seemed to turn in his heart as he remembered those days.

He walked up to the house and twisted the doorbell key, listening to the strident echo within the house, and the sound of it took him back a full seven years, and for a moment he almost thought he had never been away.

He saw a woman come into the hallway, and at first he thought it might be the maid. *"We have help, of course,"* Brady had said. *"It's quite too much for Ann, you know."*

He narrowed his eyes. It was Ann who was coming to the door. The door swung open, and he swiftly took off his hat. "Ann," he said with a smile.

He wasn't sure if she had changed much. Her flowing ash-blonde hair was now atop her shapely head, set with an expensive but simple comb. Her figure was just as exquisite as it had ever been, set off by a dress that certainly had never been bought in Ute Crossing. She held out a hand and flashed that lovely smile of hers, and once again his thoughts back-leaped seven long years. "Jim," she said. "It's good to see you." She tilted her head to one side. "You've changed."

"You haven't, Ann," he said.

"Come in! Come in! We've so much to talk about." She led the way into the huge living room, lighted by a huge, polished Rochester hanging lamp, and at least half a dozen Argand table lamps. A fire crackled in the fireplace. She took his old sheepskin coat and faded stetson, Jim feeling somewhat ashamed of them the while, and placed them in the hall. He looked about the room. Hanging over the fireplace was the oil painting of Ann which almost looked as though it would come to life.

"Sit down, Jim," she said. "You may smoke if you like."

"Cigar?" he said with a sly grin.

She laughed. "I've gotten over that. Dad used to smoke them before he became bedridden and Brady, of course, is always receiving boxes of them from clients, friends, and admirers."

He glanced at her. She had slightly, ever so slightly, accented the word *admirers*. This time he managed to see through the facade of lovely memory and saw Ann Short as she really was, a twenty-six-year-old woman who still had her beauty, but with something a little glacial about it now. Jim lighted up a cigar from the humidor on a table and raised his eyebrows a little. Only in his plush days had he ever been able to afford a cigar like it.

"How is Ben?" she asked.

Jim shrugged. "Older looking. Perhaps you have not

noticed it. I've seen quite a few changes in people since I've returned."

"You've changed yourself. That scar, Jim. Isn't there anything you could have done to it?"

Jim passed the tips of his fingers down the disfiguring line. "There were no stitches taken in it," he said quietly. "It was a week before I reached a doctor. The man who did it meant to mark me for life if he did not kill me."

"And him, Jim? What happened to him?"

Jim dropped his hand. "I didn't have much choice," he said.

"You killed him?"

Jim nodded.

"Death seems to hover about you, Jim."

Jim eyed her. Her face was a little flushed. He looked toward a side table, set with glass decanter and wineglasses. The firelight danced against the ruby contents of the decanter. It looked like blood.

"Wine, Jim?" she said. "I have brandy too. Scotch. Rye. Bourbon. Gin."

"Sounds like the Ute House Bar," said Jim with a smile. "Scotch too?" He raised his eyebrows.

"Make your choice."

Jim blew a puff of smoke. "I'll have what you have been drinking," he said.

She flushed a little. "I don't quite know what you mean, Jim," she said quickly.

"It's getting to be a little obvious," he said.

"You never talked like that in the old days!"

He smiled. "I had no need to. I came to see Brady at his request, Ann. It was imperative. Those were Brady's words, not mine."

She walked to the side table. "Brady had to leave," she said over his shoulder. She filled two wineglasses.

Jim studied her shapely back. "Then I wouldn't have annoyed you," he said.

"You are not annoying me," she said. She turned, and the firelight brought her smooth ivory skin to warm life. "Besides, Brady told me to tell you what he had in mind."

"So?"

She placed the wineglass on the table beside Jim's chair. She did not move, looking down at him with those lovely eyes, gold-flecked, and for a moment he almost rose to take her in his arms. "Brady said I was to warn you, Jim," she said quietly.

"About what?"

"It's dangerous for you here in Ute Crossing."

Jim sipped the wine. It was excellent port. "Did Brady tell you why? Specifically, I mean."

She sat down across from him and sipped her wine in ladylike fashion, although the queer notion came to him that if he hadn't been there she'd have tossed off a glassful like a whiskey stud downing a shot of the friendly creature. "Brady said you had antagonized Van Lassen and some of Van's friends."

"I'm worried about that," he said.

"He also said Sheriff Cullin is keeping an eye on you."

"That would be nothing new for him, even after seven years. As he told me, I had never been cleared of the charge of killing Curt Crowley. Not in his book, as he stated it."

"He's a stickler, Brady says."

Ann emptied her glass and glanced surreptitiously at the decanter.

"I'll have another too," said Jim dryly.

She flushed again. She filled the glasses and sat down again, watching him with those great eyes of hers. A warmth, not entirely engendered by the port, crept through him.

"Why don't you leave Ute Crossing, Jim?" she asked.

"I haven't been here twenty-four hours," he said. He grinned. "I must admit they've been eventful hours. Too eventful. . . ."

"Where would you go if you left?" she asked.

He leaned back in his chair. "I think you know," he said. "Why are you asking me?"

She emptied half of the glass. "Some foolish notion of going to find the people of those three unfortunate men. Isn't that the idea?"

"Yes."

"What can you possibly gain by that?"

"Nothing," he said. He looked down into his glass and twirled it on its stem, watching the red port swirl high on the rim. "I wasn't thinking of gaining anything. Anything material, that is."

"Spiritual, then?"

"Perhaps."

"You have changed, then!" she said challengingly.

He looked into those eyes where a man could lose his soul. "So have you, Ann," he said.

She looked away. She knew what he meant.

Jim relighted his cigar. It was comfortable in the warm

48

room, sipping excellent wine, smoking a top-grade cigar, feeling the heat of the fire, but strangely enough the woman made him uneasy. He suddenly wanted to leave while he still had the old picture of her in his heart.

"Brady was so concerned about you," she said. Her voice slurred a little now and then. "He said there were too many people around here who still believed you had killed Curt Crowley. He said too that Ben had made enemies for clearing you."

"Ben is still here," said Jim quietly.

"Ben has powerful friends," she said. "My husband, for one. And Sheriff Cullin likes Ben, although he won't always admit it. Alfred Hitchins thinks there is no one like Ben."

"And I have no one."

"You have Brady," she said softly. "And me. . . ."

"I know that," he said. "I am leaving Ute Crossing, Ann. I *am* going to look for the people of those three men. This should make everyone satisfied, but it doesn't seem to be doing quite that. What difference does it make if I do find the people of those three men? I feel that I must do it. It's as simple as that." He emptied his glass and stood up. He had a feeling that the house was empty except for Ann and himself. The wine had warmed his blood and stirred his passion.

She studied him for a moment, almost languorously, like a purebred she-cat watching an alley tom, scornful of his breeding, but interested in his obvious masculinity. "There's no need to get angry or to leave," she murmured.

"I have Brady's message," he said coldly.

She passed a slim hand across her lovely column of a neck. "It's lonely here," she said. "Brady is gone much of the time. I have little in common with the women of Ute Crossing." She lifted her eyes and looked full into his, and he knew right then and there that she was practically asking for it. A half-drunken doxy in a bordello would hardly have done it any differently.

He glanced toward the door.

"We're all alone, Jim," she said.

He did not dare look at her.

"Brady won't be back for hours, perhaps not until tomorrow."

He felt the cold sweat break out on him. Damn her! He had never been a close friend of Brady Short, but he admired the man for his ability and honesty, his education and intelligence. He knew that all he had to do was turn the lamps low, or take her by the hand. The touch of her hand would loose the floodgates within him. He had never forgotten her in those damnable seven years, nor could he drive her from his mind now.

A log fell in the fireplace. The wind whispered coldly about the great house. It was now or never!

"Stay," she murmured.

He looked at her. A spark seemed to leap the gap between them. Use your head, he thought. Keep away from her. You'll never be able to live in the valley of the Ute if you start in with her where you left off so many years ago.

"Jim?"

He had changed. She had said so. Everyone had said so. Yes, he *had* changed. "Tell Brady I thank him for his warning and advice," he said, and it seemed to him as though his voice were far away, as though someone else were talking, not Jim Murdock.

"Is that all?"

"What more do you want?" he asked cruelly.

She got up slowly. "Your coat and hat are in the hall," she said icily. "Let yourself out, please."

He walked to the door and looked back at her, and the look in her eyes struck at him like a living thing of hate.

"I was planning to spend a few weeks in Denver," she said quietly. "I will likely leave in a week or so. Brady thinks I need some city life. Some shopping. A little gaiety."

"Very thoughtful of Brady," said Jim.

"I am going alone," she said. Her face flushed. "If you happen to be up that way, Jim, I'll be at the best hotel." The last words came with a rush. She turned and walked toward the side table.

He shrugged into his coat, placed his hat on his head, looked up the wide, carpeted staircase to the darkness of the second floor, and thought of the many rooms up there. Of her room, likely exquisitely feminine, a background for the lovely creature who slept there. He could almost smell the perfume of the room, the perfume of her shapely body. He opened the door and shut it quietly behind him. The stairs squeaked beneath his weight in the bitter cold.

He led the gray from the barn and stopped in the road. Swiftly and quietly he padded back to the house and up the wide stairs. He looked into the living room. She stood with her back to him, and this time she had the decanter to her lips, her throat gulping convulsively as she swilled the good port.

Jim Murdock returned to the horse and mounted it. He rode toward Ute Crossing, and he did not look back through the thick, cold darkness to that vast mausoleum of a house that harbored a corpse of love. A love that would never live again.

Chapter Six

Jim Murdock had crossed the hard-frozen Blue two days after leaving Ute Crossing. He had spent the first night in a sheepherder's abandoned shack, and the bitter, lingering cold had forced him to bring the sorrel within the shack as well, out of the freezing wind. The second night he had camped in the bottoms of an unnamed creek, with hardly an hour's uninterrupted sleep because of the cold and the distant howling of the wolves along the ridges. In those two days he had not seen another living thing, except for an occasional hawk drifting with motionless pinions against the cloudless sky like a scrap of charred paper.

He followed a faint trail down the southern slope of the foothills after leaving the Blue. The three men had camped there for a month, according to what he had learned, before heading northeast toward Ute Crossing. There was no use in looking for their campsite and the sheepherder who had told Sheriff Cullin about them. The sheepherder wouldn't be there now. The flocks would have been driven south into the lower country for the winter.

The sun came up but shed little heat over the cold world below it. It sparkled from the crusted snow and the frozen watercourses. Far down the slope, hidden in a dark fringe of trees, the sun sparkled and glinted from something else, surmounted by a hazy, drifting cloud. Smoke. Maybe a man could get a hot meal there.

Jim shifted stiffly in the saddle. Now and then he looked behind him. Always there was the feeling that someone was watching him. It was a reaction honed by his years on the border; a sixth sense that had saved his life more than once. But there was nothing behind him except the cold landscape and the glittering of the sun on the snow and ice. He would be glad to get out into the more open country to the south.

The shifting wind trailed the smoke toward him, and he began to distinguish houses, the movements of people, the faint hum of life. It was a bigger town than he had suspected. He rode slowly up the main street and a sign caught his eye. Masterson's Freight Company. A wagonyard was beside it, with light and heavy freight wagons layered with snow. From a huge corral behind the building came the bawling of a mule. Steam rose from the corral and the sheds, mingling with the smoke from the chimneys.

Jim dismounted in front of a small restaurant. A boy plodded by. "What's the name of this place, son?" asked Jim.

"Meadows," said the urchin. "Useta be Masterson's Meadows, but people jus' call it Meadows now."

Jim flipped him a dime. "Is there a hock shop here?"

The kid grinned. "You down on your luck, mister? You kin have the dime back if you are."

Jim grinned back. "No. The dime is yours."

The kid pointed up the street. "You see that buildin' down there? The one leanin' over a little like it's all tired out? That's the Jew's place. Sam buys and sells anything. Anything, I tell you!"

Jim ate in the restaurant and took the sorrel to the livery for a feed. It was almost noon when he crossed the street to the curiously leaning structure. While he had eaten he had put two and two together. Gil was a lousy speller. He had written Maddows instead of Meadows . . . *Masterson's* Meadows. He had mentioned not getting a job with a man named Masterson.

Jim opened the door and walked into a weird wonderland of a vast accumulation of anything and everything he could think of. Shelving ran from floor to ceiling, crammed with all kinds of odds and ends. Boxes cluttered the floor, filled to the brims with oddments. Wires had been strung from one side of the long building to the other, and from the wires hung pots and pans, whips, harness fittings, housewares of all kinds, including a row of elegant chamber pots. The bell stopped tinkling on its big coiled spring.

"You are wanting to buy or sell, maybe?" a soft voice asked.

A derby hat seemed to rise by itself from behind a rampart of dusty sacks of feed. A wizened face studied Jim with a pair of the softest brown eyes he had ever seen outside of a doe.

"I'm looking for Sam," said Jim.

"Speaking," said the little man.

Jim walked to the rampart and looked over to see an immense rolltop desk, the pigeonholes crammed with papers, the top inches deep in forms of one kind or another. A parrot hung in a cage over the desk. "The drinks are on you, stranger!" he squawked.

"That's the story of my life," said Jim with a smile.

"You are wanting to buy? To sell? Maybe you want to buy the business? A partner I couldn't use."

Jim shook his head. "I'm afraid I'd get lost in here, Sam."

"So? I've been lost in here for ten years. What can I do for you?"

Jim shoved back his hat and felt for the makings. He offered them to Sam, and the little man shook his head. "I got a cough," said Sam. "I came west from Pittsburg to get rid of it. I should smoke? Crazy I'd be!"

Jim rolled a cigarette and lighted it. "I'm looking for information on a man named Gil," he said.

"You're a lawman?"

Jim shook his head. "He hasn't done anything," he said. He half closed his eyes. "That isn't right either."

"You are talking riddles."

Jim blew a smoke ring. "A few days ago a man by that name was lynched in Ute Crossing with two other men."

"The men what killed Mr. Crowley," said the merchant.

Jim nodded. "I found a letter in his pocket written to a woman named Sarah, but there was no address. He mentioned being here in Meadows and that he had hocked his rifle and saddle to a Jewish merchant here."

There was no expression on Sam's face.

"Do you have the rifle and saddle?" asked Jim.

"I might have."

Jim studied the little man. "There's no trouble in this for you, Sam."

"How do I know?"

"Because I tell you so."

Sam eyed the hard gray eyes, the disfiguring scar, the outthrust jaw of the big man. "I believe you," he said. He walked around the desk and brought back a Sharps-Borchardt rifle which he placed on the rampart of sacks. He went back and hauled out a good-looking saddle which he just managed to lift to a place beside the rifle.

"Can I look at them?" asked Jim.

"Be my guest," said Sam. He sat down in his swivel chair and watched Jim.

The saddle was a rim-fire hull made by Pearson of El Paso. Gil had not exaggerated when he had said he had hocked his "good saddel" in Maddows.

"A hundred-dollar saddle on a forty-dollar horse," said Sam quietly.

Jim nodded. Gil had likely worked in Texas, for the rim-fire or double-rigged hull was a favorite down that way. In this state the favorite was the Pueblo, made by either Gallup or Frazier, built more for rugged country and topping rough horses than for roping, where one had to be in and out of the saddle a lot. He had never heard Gil speak, so he couldn't tell if he had been a Lone Star stater.

The single-shot rifle was somewhat unusual, hardly the type to be carried as a saddle gun like the handy, quick-firing Winchester repeater. Jim checked the caliber. It was the government .45/70 with double-set trigger.

"A good rifle?" asked Sam.

Jim nodded.

"How much is it worth, maybe?"

Jim shrugged. "Fifteen dollars."

Sam paled a little. "I loaned him twenty-five on it. He didn't want to part with it, so I figured it was maybe worth something."

"You're all heart, Sam," said Jim.

"I know it," the little man said sadly.

"The drinks are on you, stranger!" squawked the parrot.

Jim examined the rifle. It was dented here and there, scratched quite a bit, but mechanically perfect. There were no identifying marks on it other than the maker's name and serial number.

There was a screwdriver lying on a table. Jim picked it up and removed the butt plate from the rifle. "Gil Drinkwater," he read. "Eighteen seventy-eight. Las Cruces."

"You're a clever fellow," said Sam. "In a hundred years I wouldn't have thought of that."

Jim replaced the butt plate. "Will you keep the saddle and rifle until I send for them?"

Sam shrugged. "Why not? Business is lousy. You wouldn't consider maybe buying me out?"

"Not today."

"The drinks are on you, stranger!" shrieked the parrot.

Sam stood up and watched Jim roll a cigarette. "You are maybe looking for the next of kin?"

Jim lighted up and then nodded.

"Why?"

Jim blew a smoke ring. "Someone has to do it," he said.

54

"He's got a wife, maybe? A family?"

"Someone named Sarah, Sam."

"A good Yiddish name."

"Did he come in here alone?" asked Jim.

"Yes."

"He was supposed to get a job with Masterson."

Sam nodded.

"Why didn't he get it?"

Sam rubbed his jaw. "About the dead I would not talk."

"Booze?"

Sam looked up. He nodded. "So drunk he was I didn't even want to take his goods, but he was desperate. You understand?"

"Yes."

Sam waved a hand. "He did not look like the kind of man who would kill an old man for money. Why, he didn't even have a gun when he left here, friend."

Jim looked up quickly from the rifle. "No belt gun?"

Sam shook his head. "I saw him ride from town with those two other fellows. A Mexican-looking fellow and a kid, a *boychik*. Someone said they were heading north to look for work. A strange trio, I thought. A drunkard, a sad-looking Mexican, and a scared-looking kid."

"You don't know anything about them?"

"No. We heard about the lynching last night. A mail carrier brought the news. A terrible thing for men to take justice into their own hands."

Jim nodded.

Sam leaned forward. "I'll keep the saddle and rifle for you. This woman. This Sarah. She has maybe no money?"

"Gil had written her that he would send for her when he had money and a job."

The sad doe eyes studied Jim. "Wait," said Sam. He vanished behind the desk. A door opened and closed. A few minutes later it opened and closed again. Sam reappeared. He handed Jim a wad of bills. "For the lady," he said.

Jim counted it. There were a hundred dollars in the wad. He whistled. "A lot of money, Sam. Maybe I'll take it and go off on a high lonesome."

The little man shrugged. "If you need a high lonesome, friend, more than Sarah needs the money, you go right ahead."

Jim grinned. "You're all right, Sam."

Sam shook his head. "It is you that is all right."

Jim walked to the door, followed by Sam. Jim turned and held out a hand.

55

The little man gripped it. "You will stop by on your way back, maybe? It was a pleasure doing business with you."

"The name is Murdock. Jim Murdock of Ute Crossing. I'll stop by, Sam, and let you know about Sarah. It might be a long time."

Sam smiled sadly. "What else do I have but time?"

Jim opened the door. The bell tinkled.

"The drinks are on you, stranger!" shrieked the parrot.

Sam shrugged. "He used to belong to a barkeeper. He ain't much company, but at least he talks to old Sam."

"Adios, Sam."

"Good-bye, Jim."

The bell tinkled as the door was closed behind Jim.

Jim crossed the border into New Mexico Territory at noon and camped that night in a ruined stone house in the valley of the San Juan. He reached Bernalillo four days later, put the sorrel into a freight car, and rattled down the valley of the Rio Grande to Socorro, where the railroad turned west. Then he crossed the old Jornado del Muerto in the bright winter sunlight, ninety waterless miles to San Diego Mountain, where he took the well-traveled road into Las Cruces. He took a room in the old Amador Hotel; its rooms still had marked over the doors the names of the girls —La Luz, Maria, Esperanza, Natalia, Dorotea, Muneca, and others, twenty-three in all—who had served the officers from Fort Selden to the north and Fort Fillmore to the south in the old days. Where were they now? thought Jim. La Luz, Maria, and the others. Perhaps respectable dowagers, happily married to the young men who had patiently waited for their future brides to earn their doweries in the big bedrooms of the Amador.

Three days of questioning brought no information about Sarah. He tried first with the name Gil Drinkwater, and found that most of the bartenders remembered Gil all too well. He had been cut off many times by every one of them. Sarah? They didn't know. The only lead he got was the fact that Gil had written infrequent letters to someone in Ysleta, a few miles southeast of El Paso. Jim knew the town well, having served for a time with the Frontier Battalion of the Texas Rangers, C Company, which had its headquarters in Ysleta, but he had never known anyone by the name of Sarah Drinkwater.

A cold drizzle was turning the streets of Las Cruces into pasty, gray-white mud when he headed toward the Amador after checking out his gear, for he meant to leave the next morning for El Paso and points south. Here and there he caught glimpses of yellow light behind shuttered windows. He stopped in a doorway to light a cigar, his mind filled with thoughts, and as he raised his head and looked up he saw a man move swiftly into another deep doorway across the street. Jim winced as the match burned his fingertips. He lowered the cigar and held it behind him while he peered toward the dark doorway. There was no movement. Casually he thrust the cigar into his mouth and walked toward the next street, rounding the corner, then running as swiftly and as silently as possible to an alleyway. He darted into it, vaulted a low, crumbling adobe wall, cursing softly as his boots sank into the soft, odorous filth of someone's pigsty, then floundered across it to a gate set between two buildings. He walked swiftly toward the next street and stopped behind a sagging two-wheeled cart, peering between the rough slats so that his hat might not be silhouetted.

Boots thudded against the street, and a tall, broad-shouldered man passed the entrance of the alley. Jim padded to the mouth of the alley and looked up the narrow, twisting street. The man stood in front of a dimly lighted shop, also looking up the street. He turned as someone opened the shop door, letting a flood of yellow light into the wet street. His features were plain to be seen—a beak of a nose, a thick dragoon moustache, shaggy eyebrows that almost met over the deep-set eyes. "Lyss," said Jim to himself. There was no mistaking the man. Jim faded back into the darkness as Lyss walked toward the alley.

Jim unbuttoned his coat as an icy feeling poured through his body. He drew his Colt. A stream of cold water struck the back of his hat and flowed freely down his back. Boots squelched in the pasty mud of the street, and then the sound died away. This was no sheer coincidence, Jim thought. Lyss was looking for him, following him for some definite purpose. But why? It couldn't be a personal reason. Jim had not known the man in the old days, and he hadn't spoken to him when he had returned to Ute Crossing. But Lyss had seemed to be closer to Van Lassen than any of the other lynchers; about as close as any man could get to Lassen. Whatever Lyss had come to Las Cruces for prophesied no good to Jim Murdock.

Jim eased his way behind the cart. Boots squelched again, then stopped, then sounded again. Jim saw the wet back of Lyss's coat not two feet from him. Even as he looked, Lyss turned. Lyss opened his mouth. Jim's Colt barrel cracked alongside his head, but the heavy, wet brim of the hat saved the man from being coldcocked. Lyss staggered sideways, clawing for his Colt. He freed it. A knee came up into his groin. He grunted in agony. Once again the Colt barrel slapped at the side of his head, this time drawing blood from beneath the dark hair. Lyss swung wildly with his own Colt. The front sight traced a faint course down Jim's right cheek. Before the man could fire Jim kneed him again, and as his head came down in reflex the Colt barrel smashed across the base of his neck, driving his beak of a nose into the foul mud of the alleyway. He groaned once and lay still.

Jim padded to the mouth of the alley. No one was in sight. The shop lights were out. Jim wiped the blood from his face with the back of a hand and went back to Lyss. He rolled the man over, and wide, staring eyes looked up into his, but they did not see, nor would they ever see again.

Jim stood up, cursing softly. He had not meant to kill the man, but he knew as sure as fate that Lyss had meant to kill him. There was no time to stand there meditating about it. Perhaps Lyss had not come alone. Swiftly Jim ripped open Lyss's coat and took out his wallet. He took the bills from it, and the papers as well. He took the muddy Colt and thrust it into his coat pocket. He rolled the heavy body beneath the cart. If anyone found Lyss within the next day or so, they'd not be able to identify him, and if Jim could get clear of Las Cruces that night, it was possible he'd not be associated with the man's killing. Distasteful as his actions were, he knew he would have received the same treatment from Lyss.

Jim wiped the blood from his face again. He retreated the same way he had come. He had left word at the Amador that he would leave before dawn. There would be no one around to check what time he had left. He gathered his gear and left by the back way, walking to the stable where a hostler slept the deep sleep of the just. Jim tucked a bill into the man's shirt pocket and got the sorrel. He rode south on the El Paso road through the slanting rain. Ten miles from Las Cruces he dropped the empty wallet and the Colt into the well of an abandoned adobe. The bills he had placed in his own wallet. He ripped Lyss' papers to bits, letting the rain-laden wind scatter them through the muddy fields. He looked back through the darkness. A strange thought flitted through his mind. *Those who live by the sword . . .*

Chapter Seven

Ysleta dozed a little in the bright sunlight that had followed the two-day rainstorm that had swept across lower New
Mexico and West Texas. The air was fresh and clear, with
a few puffs of clouds in the blue sky. The crisp ringing of a
sledge upon metal came from a blacksmith's shop, mingled
with the insistent braying of a mule.

The tall Yanqui rode into town on a tired, mud-splashed
sorrel. There were always such horsemen on the road, and
what they did or where they went was of little moment to
the people of Ysleta. There was never any serious trouble
in Ysleta. There was a good enough reason. A company of
level-eyed, quiet-spoken gentlemen known as Texas Rangers
had their headquarters there.

Now and then these tall horsemen would look back over
their shoulders as though expecting to see someone following them. This, too, was not unusual. It was better, senor,
for a man to mind his own business, you understand, for
if the stranger did not bother you, why bother the stranger?

This stranger was not one to be trifled with or stared at,
for the thin scar on his left cheek and the hardness of his
gray eyes were the stamp of his breed. He was better left
to his master, likely El Diablo.

Jim Murdock found Sarah's little adobe easily. In such a
town everyone knew everyone else. The adobe had a neat
garden in front of it, and a cat dozed on a chair in the sun.
Jim tethered the sorrel to the fence and opened the creaking gate. A woman opened the blue-painted door of the
adobe as Jim walked toward the house. Jim took off his hat.

She narrowed her pale blue eyes. "You've come about Gil,"
she said quietly.

"Mrs. Drinkwater, ma'am?" asked Jim.

She was as plain as a fence post and as gaunt as a Joshua
tree, with a rather long face, almost horselike in appearance,
and the faint trace of a moustache showed on her lined
upper lip. Her sparse hair was almost iron gray in color,
drawn tightly back over her head. Her dress was black,

59

with no adornment save a simple gold pin over her shallow breasts. All in all, hardly a woman a man would love, and yet the last lines of Gil's letter came back to Jim, almost as though imprinted on his mind. *"I say goodbye now and send you my best wishes, and be patent for I will soon have good work and scratch for both of us my dear Sarah."*

"Where is he?" she asked.

Jim hesitated. "My name is Jim Murdock," he said. "From up north. Ute Crossing."

There was no recognition in her pale eyes. "What is it you have to tell me?" she asked.

She didn't know. . . . She didn't know, but she expected the worst. . . .

"Please come in, Mr. Murdock," she said. "It was impolite of me to keep you standing here."

The living room was sparsely furnished but neat and clean. A large sewing basket stood on a chair beside a rather ancient Howe sewing machine. "You must excuse this mess," she said with a faint smile. "You must understand that this is my place of business as well as being my home." She sat down in a rocker, straight backed, thin, worn hands folded in her lap. A plain gold wedding band showed on her left hand.

"You didn't know he was at Ute Crossing, ma'am?" asked Jim.

"The last letter I had from him came from Albuquerque," she said. "He had had a promise of a job further north. A place called Maddows, I believe."

"Meadows," said Jim. "Masterson's Meadows."

She smiled that faint, mirthless smile. "I taught Gil how to read and write," she said. "I never could teach him how to spell and punctuate."

Jim wet his lips. He looked about. This was going to be worse than he had anticipated.

"You may smoke," she said.

"Thanks, ma'am." Jim rolled a cigarette and lighted it. He drew in the smoke gratefully.

"He's dead, isn't he?" she said. She nodded. "You wouldn't have come this long distance for any other reason."

Jim nodded. "You might never have found out," he said quietly. "I thought you should know."

"How did he die, Mr. Murdock?"

This was worse than admitting Gil was dead.

"You may tell me, Mr. Murdock. I will find out someday, in any case."

"He was taken from the Ute Crossing jail by an armed mob," said Jim. He could go no further.

"Shot?" she said softly, very softly.

He twisted the brim of his hat in his big hands. "He was hanged, ma'am," he said at last. He did not dare to look at her.

"Why?" she asked.

He managed to look at her. "He and two other men murdered Cass Crowley, a prominent rancher and a political power in the state. If it had been a lesser known person Gil might still be alive with a chance for his life. Believe me, Mrs. Drinkwater, there were men in Ute Crossing who did their best to save him and the others. The sheriff went all the way to the governor for a change of venue. It was while he was gone that the mob took justice into their own hands!"

There was a long silence. The thin hands worked a little. She was a lady, of good breeding, and she would not break down. The curious thought came into Jim's mind that she must have been a strange contrast to Gil and his rough ways. She had been educated.

"He was lynched, then?" she said suddenly in a clear voice. "My Gilbert was lynched?"

Dear God, thought Jim, *why did it have to be me that told her this news?*

"He meant to send for me," she said. "Somehow I knew he never would. That he would never come back."

Jim walked to the door and got rid of the suddenly tasteless cigarette. It was time to finish his business and leave her. There were others who had to be told. He wondered now if he could go through this experience two more times. He gently opened the thin hands and placed the badly written letter in them. "There was some money," he said.

She did not answer.

Jim took out his wallet. To the hundred Sam had given him he added the seventy-five dollars he had found in Lyss' wallet and added another hundred of his own. He placed the money on the side table beside the basket of sewing. "His saddle and rifle are up north," he said. "I can have them sent to you, if you like."

She shook her head. "Please accept them as compensation for your services."

"It's a fine saddle," he said.

"Yes. Gil wouldn't part with it for anything."

"No," lied Jim.

She looked up at Jim. "He had always been in trouble before we met in Amarillo," she said. "But those days were over. He only carried that rifle to shoot game when he needed it."

Jim studied her. "No belt gun? No six-shooter?"

She shook her head. "Gil never carried such a weapon. Not for many years."

"May I ask why?"

"Gil drank a lot. Years ago he accidentally killed his best friend in a drunken shooting match." She looked away. "Gil was a crack shot. When he was sober he'd win shooting matches with that rifle of his. He and his friend were shooting tin cups from each other's heads. Gil missed. He was exonerated, but he never carried a six-shooter again, and would only carry a single-shot rifle. It was a sort of taboo for him to have more than one cartridge. If he had stayed away from drink it would have been all right." She smiled. "I altered that."

"You stopped his drinking, then?" he asked.

She looked up. "Yes. They said I couldn't do it. He was a fine man when he wasn't drinking, Mr. Murdock." She narrowed her eyes. "Was he drinking up north?"

"No," lied Jim.

She stood up. "You want to leave," she said. "I don't blame you." She walked with him to the door. "How did Mr. Crowley die?"

"Shot through the back of the head. Three bullets. Forty-four caliber. Pistol bullets. They say each of the murderers had one empty shell in his six-gun when they were captured."

She placed a hand on his arm. "Then it was not Gil who was guilty," she said firmly. "He never carried such a weapon."

Gil Drinkwater had not been carrying a belt gun when he had been in Meadows. According to Sam, Gil didn't have any weapon at all, at least no gun of any kind. He could have picked up another, or borrowed one from the Mexican or the kid, who had been with him when Crowley was murdered.

"They did take care of his body?" she asked.

He nodded. "One of the leading citizens of the town paid for the burials," he said.

"Perhaps someday I will come and see his grave," she said.

"Perhaps you'd like to have his body brought down here," he said.

"No. He had no one who cared about him beyond me."

"I can't always have bad luck Sarah and you know no one

62

to home will give me a job because of the old days which are long gone and won't never come back I tell you. . . ."

She looked up into his face. "Let him stay with the two men with whom he died," she said. "They will have something in common, at least. They will be together. Good-bye, Mr. Murdock. It was kind and generous of you to let me know."

He walked to the gate without looking back and untied the sorrel. He mounted and rode swiftly away.

He was gone half an hour before she looked at the money for the first time, and she knew in her heart of hearts that Gil Drinkwater had never left her *that* much money.

It was Sergeant Les Gilson of C Company, Frontier Battalion, Texas Rangers, who gave Jim a possible tip-off on where the people of the man named Orlando might be found. Gilson's strong, tobacco-stained fingers poked through Orlando's relics. "This button is from a Mex Army uniform," he said. He checked the inside of the watch as Jim had done. "Looks like a presentation watch for some kind of service. Won by a Teniente Teodoro something or the other. At Colonia someplace or another. There are a lot of *colonias* in Mexico, Jim."

Jim turned over the faded picture. "San Fed . . ." he said.

Gilson nodded. "Possibly San Fedro or San Federico."

"You know of such a place?"

Gilson pulled down a detailed roller map of the border country, and then one of the State of Chihuahua in northern Mexico. He studied it for a moment. "Let me see that watch again," he said. He opened it and took a powerful magnifying glass from a drawer, studying the engraved script that had been scored through. "Eighteen seventy-two," he said at last.

Jim nodded. "Just as I suspected," he said. "The Mex must have stolen it. He was too young to have earned such an award that many years ago as a *teniente* in the Mexican Army."

Gilson snapped shut the watch. "About 1872 there was a helluva big Apache raid down into Chihuahua. A small force of Mexican soldiers fought them to a standstill and defeated them. There weren't many Apaches left alive after the fracas, and hardly enough soldiers left to bury the dead." He eyed the map. "The little *placita* where the Mexes held off the Apaches was abandoned by the people who had lived there because of the curse on it."

Jim rolled a cigarette and handed the makings to Gilson.

Gilson fashioned a smoke and lighted it. "By God!" he said. "That place was called Colonia Federico!"

Jim took the cigarette from his mouth. "You're sure about that, Les?"

The ranger nodded. "It's down near Laguna de Haros. There's nothing left down there now, Jim, except mounded graves and ruined dobes. I passed through that country some years ago on an undercover scout. You're wasting your time going down there."

Jim gathered together the relics of the man named Orlando. "It's enough of a lead to warrant a little time down there."

Gilson shook his head. "Beats the hell out of me," he said. "You were one helluva fine ranger, Jim, although I always did say you thought too much, too deep."

Jim grinned. "My mother used to say that about me." He gripped the sergeant's hand. "Much obliged, Les. I've found the kin of one of those poor men. I feel it is an obligation to find the others."

Les flipped his cigarette butt into a garboon. "Where'd you find the first of them?" he asked.

Jim looked Les full in the eyes. "It doesn't really matter, does it, Les?"

Les shook his head. "I understand," he said.

The ranger watched Jim leave the headquarters building and lead the tired sorrel toward a livery stable. "Four hundred miles to tell the kin of a murdered man that he has died. Now he's riding south more than a hundred miles to do it again, *if* he can find the kin of the second murderer. I still think you think too much and too deep, Jim Murdock, but it's your life, and I know better than to tell you different."

Jim crossed the Rio Grande on a flatboat ferry to Zaragoza the day after he reached Ysleta, riding a chunky dappled gray he had traded the crippled sorrel for, plus twenty-five in cash. He had no desire to stay too long in Ysleta. There was extradition between New Mexico and Texas, of course, but none between those places and Mexico. They would have found the body of Lyss by now, and the law in Las Cruces and Dona Ana County might be more than passing interested in the man who had left the Hotel Amador in the dark of a rainy night to head south toward the border. He had registered under his own name, of course, for he had had no reason not to. If he had known he was being tailed by Lyss he would have registered under an assumed name. The damage had been done, however. The dark streets of towns along the border and near the border quite frequently yielded

64

dead men staring at the cold dawn sky with eyes that did not see, stripped of wallets and other valuables.

One thought ran constantly through his mind. Sam had said Gil Drinkwater had not carried a belt gun or rifle when he had left Meadows. That in itself meant little, for it would have been easy enough for Gil to pick up a six-gun. It was the deep sincerity of the woman Sarah, who had told him that Gil would not carry a six-shooter, which stuck in his stubborn craw. Yet Cass Crowley had died with three .44 slugs in the back of his head, which also meant little, for the shooting could have been done by one of the killers with either a rifle or a six-shooter. But the three killers had been found armed with six-guns, *and an empty cartridge case in each weapon!*

Now and then Jim would turn in his saddle and look back north as he rode, as if it might help him to penetrate the minor mystery of a man who would not carry a six-gun because of a terrible accident in his past. *"Then it was not Gil who was guilty,"* she had said firmly. *"He never carried such a weapon."*

He took the stagecoach from Villa Palmito, after selling the gray for the fare, and arrived two days later in Chihuahua at dusk. If he could find out Orlando's last name, he might possibly be able to trace the man. As it was, it took him almost a week to get the information he wanted about the siege of Colonia Federico by the Apaches, and the stout defense of the Mexican soldiers led by a Teniente Teodoro Abeyta, who, severely wounded, had been forced to retire from the army. There was no mention of anyone called Orlando, and no information about a place called San Federico in the State of Chihuahua.

He walked through the plaza his last night in Chihuahua City, ignoring the shrill-voiced boys pimping for their teenage sisters, listening instead to a deep-toned church bell which seemed to call to him. He lighted a cigar and walked slowly toward the church, watching the mantilla-clad heads of the women converging on the church. There was a small building beside the church, and an aged padre stood there, enjoying the crispness of the night air.

"Good evening to you, father," said Jim.

"And to you, my son," said the old padre. "Can I be of help to you?"

"I am looking for a place called San Federico," said Jim.

"There are likely many San Federicos." The padre smiled. "Have you no clue to locate it approximately?"

"None, except that it might be near a place called Laguna

de Haros. There was a place called Colonia Federico there some years ago, now abandoned."

The padre looked at him intently. "Yes, it comes to me now! The people there thought there was a curse upon the place. They moved, bag and baggage, as you Americans say, to another place, far to the west."

"But where, padre?"

The father held out his hands, palms upward, and shrugged his rounded shoulders. "Beyond the Sierra Vallecillos, it is said."

"Perhaps in the State of Sonora?"

"It is possible, my son." He eyed Jim. "Why do you ask?"

"There are possibly people there who would like to know of the death of a son, a father, a brother. I know nothing of the dead man except that his given name was Orlando, and that someone he knew, possibly relatives, a wife and children, perhaps, lived in a place that could either be San Fedro or San Federico."

"You know only his given name? It is a very common one."

Jim shrugged. "Perhaps it is Orlando Abeyta. There is a possible connection between this man I knew and a Teniente Teodoro Abeyta."

"Ah," said the padre in a soft voice. "Abeyta! That is better. There was an Orlando Abeyta I once knew."

"Here in this city?"

The padre nodded. "Yes, but that was many years ago." He studied Jim. "How did this man die, senor?"

"Does it matter?"

"To me it does. You see, I was once the teacher of a young man named Orlando Abeyta."

The bell stopped ringing. It was very quiet in the dark street except for the low voices in the church.

"How did he die, senor?" repeated the padre. "Not badly, I hope."

"He died like a man, padre. As he said at the last: *'It is not the thought of dying that is painful, only the way of it.'*" Jim looked steadily at the padre. "He was hanged for murder in the States, padre. You will tell no one?"

The padre's face was set and white, as though someone had struck him across it. "Hanged?" he said in a weak voice. "Orlando Abeyta hanged for murder? But this is impossible!"

"I swear it is true, padre."

"No, it cannot be. He was such a gentle lad. Brave in his own way. Not a hero like his elder brother, of course, but then Orlando had never wanted to be a soldier. Had he been

66

stronger in spirit he would have resisted all efforts to make him a soldier, except for being a soldier of God. Tell me about him, senor."

Jim quickly told his tragic story. "He was a brave man," he concluded.

"Why did you take this task upon yourself? What did this man mean to you?" asked the padre.

Jim glanced at the church. "Perhaps it is a form of penance. Perhaps an unspoken vow. I don't really know. Something made me come."

"God moves in inscrutable ways, my son."

"You do not know if he was married and had a family?"

"He once told me he would never marry."

Jim took out the faded picture and lighted a match so that the padre could see the woman and the two little children. The padre shook his head. "I believe his elder brother was married. Yes! I remember now! She was a beautiful young woman. Much younger than her husband. Somewhat older than Orlando." The padre studied the picture again. "I cannot tell. It is too faded. There is one thing I do know, and that is that Orlando Abeyta was in love when he was very young, but that it was an unrequited love."

Jim replaced the picture in his wallet. "It is said that Teniente Abeyta was severely wounded at Colonia Federico and was forced to retire because of his wounds. Perhaps, if I could find him, I could tell him of his brother's death."

"All those people moved west, my son, into the Sierra Vallecillos. The Abeytas had lived near Laguna de Haros for many generations. There are few people, if any, living there now."

Jim blew a reflective puff of smoke from his cigar. "Then my best bet is to head west into the Sierra Vallecillos to try and find the relatives of Orlando Abeyta."

"Do you know that country?"

"I've heard of it," said Jim dryly.

"It is almost impassable in places. Infested with outlaws, wild animals, marauding Apaches and Yaquis."

"It is something I have to do, padre."

The padre nodded. "I will say prayers for the soul of Orlando Abeyta," he said.

"He died a condemned man, padre. At least he was condemned by the people who hanged him."

"Do you believe he was guilty?"

"All the available evidence indicates that he was."

The padre shrugged. "It is impossible for me to believe

that he would murder a man. Continue on your quest, my son. I will say prayers for you as well."

Jim smiled. "Likely I'll need them. Good night, padre. Thanks!"

The old man watched the tall Americano walk away, cigar at a jaunty angle, booted feet striking the street steadily, arms swinging by his sides. "Yes," said the padre softly. "You will need prayers, my son. Many prayers. Go with God!" He walked into the dimly lighted church. It would be well to begin right away.

The streets were dark except for an occasional lamp flaring in the cold wind. It would be a cold, hard journey to the west into the wild country of the Sierra Vallecillos, many areas of which were marked "impassable" or "unknown," the home of the wild ones, animals, white and red men, all as wild as the country.

He was within a block of his shabby hotel when something seemed to warn him. He crossed to the other side of the dark street and worked his way toward the hotel. Two men stood on the corner in the biting wind, looking at the hotel, dark except for faint lamplight in one or two windows and in the little, dusty lobby where the clerk dozed in one of the run-down chairs.

Jim watched the two men. One of them nodded his head. He scraped a match against the nearest wall and lighted a cigarette, and in the dancing flare of the match flame Jim saw a face he knew from Ute Crossing. It was the man named Slim. The match flickered out.

Jim stepped back into a deep doorway and eased his Colt in its sheath. Once again an icy feeling surged through him, as it had that wet night in Las Cruces when he had recognized Lyss. He was a long way from Las Cruces, where Lyss had likely been buried by now. He was a much longer distance from Ute Crossing. But it wasn't too far for men from Ute Crossing to follow Jim clear down into Chihuahua.

He had registered in the Amador Hotel in Cruces under his own name, so they would know for sure he had been that far south. He had left no written record of his presence in El Paso or in Ysleta, but Sarah Drinkwater and Sergeant Les Gilson had known he had been there, a week or more ago. It would have been logical enough for anyone following him to have crossed the Rio Grande into Zaragoza to ask a few questions. Perhaps someone there would remember the tall Americano with the knife scar on his left cheek. They might have worked as far south as Villa Palmito and learned there that he had taken the stagecoach to Chihuahua City. They might have arrived a few days behind him. They weren't just standing on that windy street corner speculating on where he was staying. They damned well knew!

He waited until he had a chance to slip back down the street. It took him only a few minutes to get to the run-down livery stable where he had left the coyote dun he had bought. Most of his gear was locked up in the storeroom of the stable. A handful of centavos was enough to send a hostler back to the hotel via the back way to get the rest of Jim's gear.

The wind shifted, blowing strongly from the northwest, as Jim left the city and rode through the darkness toward Gran Morelos.

Chapter Eight

"Colonia Federico," said the gray-haired Mexican. He shoved back his heavy felt steeplehat and looked at Jim Murdock. "Why would one want to come here, senor?"

Jim hooked a leg about the pommel of his saddle, rolled a cigarette, and passed the makings to the old man. His eyes were busy taking in the long-abandoned site of the *colonia*. "One comes because one has a reason, Augustin," he said quietly. He lighted the cigarette and blew a puff of smoke that was taken away by the cold wind blowing from the north across the site of the old settlement.

"There is nothing here but ruin," said the old man. He deftly fashioned a cigarette, twisted the tip together, and accepted a light from Jim. *"Gracias,"* he said.

"Por nada," said Jim.

Augustin waved a brown, veinous old hand. "The bat and the owl, the lizard and the snake, live here. No humans will live here. It is an accursed place, senor."

"It is all in the mind, old man."

The sloe eyes of the Mexican studied Jim. "That is not so," he said quietly. "You yourself, perhaps, live under a curse?"

"Why do you ask?"

"Why would one come here? There is something in your eyes. Your voice. The way you say and do things. A man

69

who, perhaps, has a dog riding upon his back. A thing he must do? There are those under a curse who must wander on and on until the curse is lifted."

"And if it is not?"

Augustin shrugged. "Perhaps the senor knows that better than I do."

"Come, old man, let us see this place."

Augustin looked up at the sky. "It is almost dusk," he said. "There will be an early moon."

The Mexican shook his head. "There is no need to guide you, Senor Murdock. I will make the camp beyond this ridge. There is a water hole there. I will make the food."

Jim smiled. "One is not afraid?"

"Who? Me? I am not afraid, senor!"

Jim held his hands out, palms upward, smiled and shrugged. "I was but jesting, Augustin."

The old man smiled faintly. He tugged at his heavy gray moustache. "You have, perhaps, a cross? A Bible?"

Jim shook his head.

Augustin handed him a rosary. "Keep it in your hand," he said. "Senor, do not stay there after dark. . . ." He turned his mule and led the packmule up the ridge and was soon out of sight.

Jim hefted the rosary in his hand. He smiled and slipped it into his coat pocket.

The old man was right. Colonia Federico was now little more than a dusty name upon the empty landscape, soon to be completely forgotten. The home of the owl, the bat, the lizard, and the snake. There seemed to be little pattern in the humps of sand, gravel, and eroded adobe bricks that had once been houses, cantinas, shops, a small barracks and, of course, a church. Jim led the dun into the smoothly swept plaza, kept neat and tidy by the wind. By half closing his eyes he could visualize this little *placita* sleeping in the bright, hot suns of the summers, bowed beneath the bitter winter winds. Beyond the *placita* ruins he saw the vast, shallow bowl of the long-dry Laguna de Haros, which might fill up for a time during the heavy rains, or when the snow melted, although there would not be very many heavy snows.

Here it was that Teniente Teodoro Abeyta, with forty men, had held the *placita* against all the assaults of a combined force of Apaches and Yaquis, hundreds in number, it was said, who had been on their way south to strike at the gates of Parral, or perhaps even those of Durango itself. They had had no great interest in Colonia Federico save that they needed fresh meat, and there were many mules in those days

70

at the *colonia,* and the flesh of mules is sweet to an Apache or a Yaqui. Perhaps the alcalde could have dealt peacefully with the fierce warriors, the tigers of the mountains and deserts. It had been done before. The quixotic minds of the marauders might have let them take the mules and spare the inhabitants, as a sort of tribute to the fierceness and the power of the Apaches and their cousins the Yaquis. They might even have ignored the barefooted, shakoed infantry-men of Teniente Abeyta's company. This, too, had been done before. Likely the warriors were better armed than the little brown men whom they usually scorned.

But if the Apaches and the Yaquis were tigers of the mountains and deserts, there was also a tiger who had been sleeping in Colonia Federico. A man, an officer of the Mexican Army, whose blood was as proud and fierce as that of the warriors. A soldier whose fierce independence had caused his senior officer to practically bury him in Colonia Federico. His exile had done nothing to curb the spirit of Teodoro Abeyta.

No one knew to this day what had caused the spark to leap the gap from Mexican to Apache, but in the cold light of the early dawn, with the plaza filled with warriors, bands of white paint across their fierce noses and high cheekbones, the *n'deh b'keh,* the thick-soled, button-toed, thigh-length moccasins on their muscular legs, strong hands resting on rifle or lance, the spark had leaped. In the first few minutes of confused shooting Teniente Abeyta lost nine men, the Apaches six. The Apache and the Yaqui do not like hand-to-hand fighting. Their methods are those of the guerilla—the rifle shot from the mesquite, the ambush in the narrow pass, the killing of men before they have a chance to kill, then the leisurely knife and war-club work on the screaming wounded who see their deaths on the impassive brown faces of the warriors. Here, in the plaza, they had lost six good warriors. Perhaps if they had been fighting better troops, like those of the famous Indian-fighting Sixth Mexican Infantry, they might have taken their losses and retreated, for after all, they had killed more Mexicans than the Mexicans had killed warriors. But they did not retreat, and in the vicious infighting through the narrow streets of the *placita,* the Mexicans, led by Abeyta, drove the screaming warriors out to the naked land between the *placita* and the lagoon, which in those days was filled with water. Abeyta drove them out, but the price was high . . . too high, for he lost eight more men.

The blood madness came over Mexican and warrior. For two days they fought with the *heshke,* the "killing craze"

71

upon them all—the infantrymen behind their battered walls, the warriors working in close, using every scrap of cover to sharpshoot any head that appeared. Abeyta kept the frightened women and children behind the thick walls of the church. He armed every man and boy in the *placita*. He leavened the frightened civilians with his best fighting men. He was himself worth ten men.

When the warriors thought Abeyta was defeated, they charged into the plaza once more to meet Abeyta and the few men he had left. A blast of gunfire came from the church. The women and children, and the walking wounded caught the bucks in the flank with a hail of lead, and Abeyta then led his few soldiers into the melee of screaming bucks, firing a volley, then charging in with needle bayonets. Rifle butts smashed into the warriors, and when the rifles were shattered the Mexicans, masters of the knife, stayed to fight until the Apaches and Yaquis had enough. The warriors fled, although their numbers were still far greater than those of the enemy. Only a handful of the soldiers remained alive, and from beneath a heap of the contorted dead they dragged out the body of Teniente Teodoro Abeyta, riddled with wounds, more dead than alive.

The sun was dying in a welter of rose and gold in the west, and then swiftly it was gone, and as swiftly came the beginning of the night cold. In the quick rush of the darkness Jim Murdock saw the many mounded graves between the ruins of the *placita* and the empty *laguna*. He led the dun toward the graves, and as he walked the eeriness of the place suddenly came upon him. He turned and looked back, but there was nothing to see. Yet many men had died there in bloody violence, and a curse was upon this place.

There would be an early moon. Augustin would have made the camp and would have beans and tortillas ready. The old man had seemed glad to leave his granddaughter's comfortable casa in Gran Morelos to guide Jim to the west. It had been said of Augustin Galeras in the cantinas of Gran Morelos that he was *muy hombre*, still much of the man, despite his many years, and no one, senor, knew the country to the west better than he, unless perhaps it was the coyote or the eagle.

Jim sat down on a rock and smoked, listening to the wind sweeping across the desert to the north, hard at work tidying up the already immaculate and sterile neatness of Colonia Federico, or what had been Colonia Federico. With its phobia for neatness, the wind would in time sweep Colonia

Federico into its immense dustpan, and thence into the great dustbin of limbo, whence no human could ever return, even in memory. It made a big man feel damned insignificant. The desert and the mountains have a way of doing just that.

In the first faint light of the rising moon that silver-washed the low hills to the east, Jim walked about among the mounded graves. There were many of them, but most of them would be of people who had died before the great fight there. To one side, separated by a shallow ditch, he found a group of graves with a marker set among them, a yellowish-white stone set upon a rock base, cemented together. The new moon shone full upon the face of the rock and the inscription cut thereon, although wind and sharp-edged dust, rain, and snow had softened the words and partially erased some of them.

Jim shoved back his hat and studied the inscription, his lips moving silently until he got the gist of it, and then he read it aloud for the bat, the owl, the lizard, and the snake to hear, for there wasn't any other living thing to listen.

To the exalted memory of the Third Company, Fourth Provisional Regiment, of the Army of the glorious Republic of Mexico: these brave men did their duty at Colonia Federico in the face of hundreds of Apaches and Yaquis, and decisively defeated them despite the great disparity in numbers. Here are inscribed the names of the honored dead and the few living men of the Third Company, who under the command of Teniente Teodoro Abeyta wrote in heroic blood a page of Mexican history. Honor to them! Learn here a lesson, you who read this: Learn that only men who do their duty are entitled to be honored on such a monument as this. To the coward: Slink silently away! Your curse is that you will always wander, but you will never escape the memory of what you did here at Colonia Federico!

Jim slowly rolled a cigarette. The monument was unusual. The "heroic" dead and the "heroic" living had indeed been honored, although few would travel to this abandoned place to read the glorious words, and the memory of man is short even when he can read the wording on such monuments. What was unusual was that there was a thrusting reference to cowardice. The cowardice of a number of men, perhaps, but more likely of one. Jim lighted the cigarette and blew a reflective puff of smoke. He hadn't expected to learn much at Colonia Federico, but Augustin had said it was only a

73

few miles out of the way on the route to Santo Tomas in the sierra to the west.

The moonlight was beginning to flood the desert. Far across the cold wastes came the faint howling of a coyote, greeting the pallid beauty of the new moon.

Jim sat there beside the eroding monument for a long time. Bits and pieces were fitting into the puzzle that had been the fatalistic Mexican known as Orlando Abeyta. A brave man who had died ingloriously with a drunkard and a frightened boy. *"He was such a gentle lad. Brave in his own way. Not a hero like his elder brother, of course, but then Orlando had never wanted to be a soldier. Had he been stronger in spirit he would have resisted all efforts to make him a soldier, except for being a soldier of God."* Jim whirled and was on his feet, fingertips brushing the worn butt of his Colt, before he realized the voice had been only in his mind. And yet it had seemed at the moment that someone, the old padre, had spoken to Jim as he had spoken to him that night in Chihuahua City, when they had talked about Orlando Abeyta, the boy who had wanted to be a priest.

The searching wind shifted, rattling bits of gravel against the monument. The moon shone upon the ruins of Colonia Federico in an eerie silvery light, etching sharp shadows from the few walls that still stood free from the harsh embrace of the desert that was again taking over the country.

Was it indeed Orlando Abeyta, the condemned and executed murderer, who had been the coward of Colonia Federico? But his brother had been the hero of Colonia Federico. Jim withdrew the fine presentation watch from his pocket. He opened the back cover and eyed the faint inscription in the clear light of the moon. His lips wordlessly shaped the inscription. "To Teniente Teodoro . . . For heroic services rendered at Colonia . . ." He closed the back of the case and pressed the repeater button. The soft, sweet chime struck six o'clock.

The dun had strayed. Jim could hardly blame him. It had been a long day's ride to Colonia Federico across rough, cold country. He stowed away the watch and walked past the dead *placeta*, heading for the ridge. There was nothing more to be learned from the place.

He slowly walked up the ridge, his thoughts miles away. A horse nickered. He turned toward the sound. A movement in the scant brush of a hollow drew him to it. He saw a horse, and his eyes narrowed. It wasn't the dun. It was a clay-bank, saddled and with pommel and cantle packs as well

74

as filled saddlebags. He looked about. There would be no tracks on that hard ground. The horse nickered again, and when Jim turned to look at him he saw another horse further up the draw. A black, saddled and with cantle and pommel packs. Both horses had been tethered to the tough brush.

He whirled at another sound and saw the dun trotting up the slope toward the other horses. One of them whinnied. Jim met the dun and led him far down the slope into a deep arroyo, tethered him, and then unsheathed his Winchester, levering a .44/40 into the chamber. He removed his spurs and padded up the ridge again, falling belly flat on the near side of the crest, dropping his hat behind him as he wormed his way up to the top of the ridge and thrust his head between two clumps of growth to peer down the far side. The moonlight glinted from the calm surface of the water hole. A thread of smoke arose from the embers of a fire set in a ring of smoke-blackened rocks. Here and there lay packs and other gear. Three men stood there in the bright moonlight, two of them tall men, Americans, no doubt, with pistols in their hands, looking at Augustin Galeras, who stood there hatless, his white hair clear and sharp in the moonlight, and a trickle of blood glistening on his brown face as it crept from his scalp to his lined jaw.

The wind shifted and blew toward Jim from the trio of motionless men. "Where is he, greaser?" said one of the men.

"I do not know of whom you speak, senor," said Augustin.

"The big gringo! Murdock! You left Gran Morelos with him three days ago! Where is that scar-faced son of a bitch?"

Jim wet his lips. The voice was that of the man named Slim, and further, there was no mistaking his build and height, for the man was a good four inches taller than Jim's six feet even.

"Talk, damn you!" said the other man.

Jim knew him too. It was the man named Jules, another member of the lynching party.

"He has gone north," said Augustin at last. A hard hand slapped the Mexican's white head back and forth until he swayed on his feet.

"You talk, by God," said Slim, "or we'll toast your dirty feet over them coals! Where did he go? What's he aimin' to do?"

Jim stood up and Augustin saw him, but the Mexican's face did not betray what he had seen. Jim walked softly down the ridge, rifle at hip level, hammer back, fingertip pressing lightly against trigger, taking up the slack. If Slim and Jules saw him or heard him, they could kill Augustin before Jim could open fire for fear of hitting the old man.

"He has gone to Temosachic," said Augustin in a quavering voice.

"Where is that?" demanded Slim.

Jim was fifty yards away now, still too far to open fire.

"In the Sierra Vallecillos, not far from Laguna de Bavicora. He goes there to talk about mining."

Slim's hard hand slashed across Augustin's face, and bright droplets of blood glistened in the moonlight as they flew from the Mexican's slack mouth. "You lie!" yelled Slim. "That bastard ain't no miner! He's looking for someone's kin, ain't he? Name of Orlando or somethin'! Ain't he?"

Jim was twenty-five feet away now. His left boot kicked a stone. "Drop!" yelled Jim to Augustin. As the old man hit the ground the two Americans whirled. Jim fired once into Jules' lean gut, and the two-hundred-grain slug doubled the man up and drove him back against Slim as though a mule had kicked him. Jim had jumped sideways as soon as he had fired, slamming the Winchester lever up and down and firing the instant the lever closed home. Slim cursed. He shoved the falling Jules aside and slapped out two rounds. Something plucked at Jim's left sleeve. He reloaded and charged directly toward the cursing man slamming out round after round. Slim went down on one knee, game, though wounded, and raised his six-shooter for his last shot. Echoes slammed back and forth between the ridges.

Augustin rolled to his feet like a cat, and something glittered in his hand as he closed in on Slim. Slim turned and struggled to his feet. The old man was in under the smoking six-shooter and the knife sank deep into Slim's hard-muscled gut, and then, with a terrible, wrenching pull across the belly and down into the soft groin, a figure seven stroke, Augustin finished the job.

Slim dropped the hot six-shooter, clutching his opened belly. He looked at Jim with terrible, staring eyes. Jim raised the rifle and fired once, right between the eyes, and Slim fell at Augustin's feet and lay still. Slowly the moon-whitened ground beneath him began to turn black from the soaking of the flood of blood.

The echoes died, fleeing off into the grim silence of the watching hills. The stench of acrid smoke hung in the draw between the moon-washed ridges.

Augustin bent on one knee and calmly wiped the bloody knife on Slim's coat. He stood up and looked at Jim. "I did not tell them," he said proudly.

76

"You did well, old one," said Jim quietly.

Augustin sheathed the blade. He spat on the two bodies. Jim wiped the cold sweat from his face. It had been a near thing.

"Why do they seek you, Jaime?" asked the old man. He studied Jim with narrowed eyes.

"I have done nothing to them," said Jim. "It seems to be something that they helped do to others that makes such men follow me." He looked about. "This is a bad thing. The killing of two Americanos here in your country."

Augustin picked up his sweat-stained old hat. He looked sideways at Jim. "Who is to know?" he said softly. He smiled. "As I said before: Only the bat and the owl, the lizard and the snake, live here."

"You said something else, old man," said Jim.

"Eh?"

Jim looked at him. "It is an accursed place. . . ."

"That is true." Augustin looked at the fire. "The meal is ready." He laughed. "They did not touch my beans or tortillas, Jaime."

"You would eat here?" asked Jim.

Augustin walked to the fire and pulled free the blackened clay pot of beans. He looked back at Jim, his great eyes peering beneath his wide, upturned hat brim. "Those two will not share our food," he said. "There is more than enough for two of us, but not enough for four. Come! Eat! We will get rid of them and hide them so not even God can find their bodies. So, then, what is to fear? *Los muertos no hablan.* . . ."

Jim nodded. The dead do not speak. It was enough. They would have killed Jim and the old man as well if they had had the chance.

There was moonlight aplenty for the ride west, after the bodies had been buried and the gear hidden. There were no brands on the two horses. Augustin picketed them lightly not far from the water hole. In time they would break free, but by then Jim and his guide would be many miles into the looming mountains.

They took the dim trail toward Santo Tomas in the last hours of the cold moonlight. Jim looked back at the dreary, godforsaken site of Colonia Federico. He had left three dead men behind him on his quest for the kin of the three men who had been hanged at Ute Crossing. Perhaps a poetic justice, for he was almost sure that there had been much more behind those lynchings than just the outraged feelings of the hard men of the valley of the Ute. Something dark

77

and evil, so evil he did not want to think about it. Not yet, anyway; not that night, for a certainty.

As they entered the first gateway into the quiet hills a coyote broke voice far in the lonely distance.

Chapter Nine

The high peaks of the Sierra Madre were snow-clad, serene and distant, as though belonging to another world. Always they looked down impassively into the terribly deep barrancas and the timbered mesas, covered with spruce and pine and red-hued madronas. They seemed not to notice the antlike creatures that walked upon two legs or rode upon larger antlike creatures with four legs. These antlike beings came and went during the centuries on some meaningless business of their own, and although they changed over the years, they were always the same to the peaks of the Sierra Madre.

For days and then weeks Jim Murdock had waited in a tiny village in a valley far below those stupendous mountains, while old Augustin Galeras struggled with life and death. In the weeks that the old man and Jim had worked their way upward into the mountains, Jim had grown to like, then to respect, and then to love the old man. He would never return to Gran Morelos. Jim knew that and Augustin knew that. A bad fall from his mule had broken many of his ribs. He had broken ribs before, but then he had been a much younger man. Still, as he had always done, he fought, but this time he fought against the one enemy who could never be defeated by man.

The old year had slipped away with hardly a murmur into the past. The mountains didn't care. The simple mountain people seemed to care less. This was a world far removed from dates and places. How could one feel important with those mountains watching him with half-lidded eyes all day?

They buried old Augustin in a grave punched out of re-sisting earth on a shelf that overlooked the brawling stream, with a good view of the great peaks. Jim Murdock had wanted to leave then, but a great norther had swept across the Sierra Vallecillos and carried with it a weight of snow that recapped the peaks, bringing the white mantles lower than anyone living in the village could ever remember, even old Santiago Esquivel, of whom it was said that he had lived in those mountains longer than the Devil himself. The snow choked the narrow passes and filled the canyons and barrancas, until, Body of God, it seemed as though no one would ever again get in or out of the lonely, almost forgotten valley.

Yet, no one really wanted to leave, and cared less about anyone coming into the valley. Even the big gringo, the gaunt man with the scar upon his face, and the big brown hands that carved such wonderful toys for the boys and girls, seemed to care little. If there was anything broken in the village he fixed it. If a horse, a goat, or a burro became ill, he knew how to treat it, and he even could treat the human sick with the little store of medicines he carried with him.

He kept his two well-oiled guns in their worn sheaths in the little hut he had shared with the old man before the old man had died. The simple villagers would surreptitiously eye that disfiguring scar on the Americano's face, the stubborn set of the strong jaw, and those steady, penetrating eyes, eyes so light in color, to the villagers, at least, that they seemed almost disfiguring. Those eyes could be as hard as granite, and yet when the Americano helped the sick or comforted a child, they would soften marvelously. They had seen him use that heavy rifle to bring down deer and bear at incredible ranges.

In the third month of the new year the big Americano rode from the village on the soft trails, guided by a silent mozo, a tribeless Tarahumare who spoke no English and very little Spanish but who knew those mountains as few other men did. Yet, not even the mozo had heard of San Federico, and not even old Santiago Esquivel himself had heard of it.

The mozo parted company with Jim at the junction of the Rio Yaqui and the Rio Moctezuma and faded away into the mountains. In two weeks he had not spoken a word to Jim.

Jim had been away from Ute Crossing for many months now. He was on a long, long trail to which there seemed to be no ending. He could not quit. *"There are those under a curse who must wander on and on until the curse is lifted."* Those had been the wise words of old Augustin Galeras to Jim Murdock. Since the deaths of Slim and Jules, Jim had heard nothing about Ute Crossing before the mountain trails

79

had been blocked, stopping even the hardy monthly mail runner. Nothing. It had been as though he had moved into another world once he and the old man had left Santo Tomas.

The days faded into weeks, and the mountain world grew warm as Jim patiently worked his way through the mountains as far west as La Colorado on the road to Hermosillo, as far south as the Sierra Baroyeca, thence east into the Rio Mayo country, then back again to the Sierra Baroyeca, to Esperanza, and up the Rio Yaqui to Tecoripa and thence north to Nacozari and Bacoachi, thence south again and east to the wild Rio Escondido. There *was* no San Federico. There never *had* been a San Federico. Perhaps there never *would* be a San Federico, senor. *Quién sabe?* Who knows? The phrase echoed in his ears in the lonely camps and in the little *placitas* and mining camps, on the twisting trails and beside the calm waters of the *lagunas*. The spring had shifted into the early summer, and still he had progressed no further than he had been when he had entered those great mountains with old Augustin Galeras so many months ago and had paid the blood price for the passage with the life of the old man. Stranger than the unknown San Federico was the complete lack of knowledge of the name of Abeyta. It seemed as though that name had never been known in those wild and forbidding mountains.

With the coming of the summer came dark news. The Chiricahua Apaches had raided down as far as Casa Blanca. The notorious Streeter Gang of half-breeds, pure quill Apaches, and renegade whites had struck in the vicinity of Fronteras. Bandits haunted the roads between the border and Hermosillo and ranged as far east as the San Miguel. Hard times, hard times indeed, senor, had come to Sonora.

Not far from Magdalena was a good spring where Jim Murdock, the gringo with the curse upon him, would camp when he was in that vicinity, resting his horse and his pack burro, letting them get fat again, although no amount of food or resting would layer fat upon the tall Americano's muscular body, gaunt from too many months on the trail that had no ending.

He approached the spring one early summer evening, an unlit Mexican cigar stuck in the corner of his mouth, the dust of the trail thick upon his animals, his clothing, and his own tanned flesh. He had seen smoke rising from the spring area on his slow climb up toward the spring from the desertlike country below. He was within a quarter of a mile of the spring when he noticed that the smoke had thickened, and the shifting breeze of the oncoming darkness brought with it the smell of burning cloth and something else he recognized, and as he recognized it, he dropped from his horse, slapped it on the rump, and jerked his Winchester from its saddle scabbard as he did so.

He drifted like a cloud shadow across the dry ground and into the shelter of rocks and scrub trees. The wind shifted again, and he was positive of the odor that came with it. Burning flesh. . . . There was only one possible source for *that* odor. It was a favorite device of Apaches and Yaquis to use fire on their victims.

The horse had led the docile pack burro into the shelter of the trees down the slope, unseen if anyone looked down from the spring area. Jim worked his way through the trees and tumbled boulders until he could belly forward to overlook the spring. Years ago someone had built a rock house there, but now the roof had partially tumbled in and one of the walls had collapsed. The spring was beyond the house in a great cup of sun-bleached rocks. The thickening smoke rose from a fire at the edge of the rocks where a man, a Mexican by his clothing, lay sprawled on his back across the coals, his arms outflung and his face a red mask of blood. Beyond him lay another man, more likely a big boy, doubled up, with a dark stain on the back of his shirt. A mule, tethered to a tree, was fighting the rope that tied him to the tree.

Jim wet his dry lips, studying the scene with slitted eyes. There were others down there somewhere. He was sure of it. He looked back over his shoulder to make sure he wasn't being flanked. There was no one there.

Suddenly a woman screamed, and Jim's head snapped around. He raised his rifle. She had come staggering out from the old house, holding rags of clothing about her almost naked body, running across the empty ground toward the spring. A man stood up from among the rocks, his steeple-crowned hat on the back of his head, a grin on his brown face, and his arms outstretched to catch this ripe plum of femininity. She darted sideways and ran down the slope. Two more men appeared from the brush, grinning at her, their white teeth in sharp contrast to their dusty moustaches and dark skins. One of them snatched at her rags, and as she pulled away she stood there trembling, mother-naked, trying to cover her full breasts with her arms, while the three men roared with drunken laughter.

Jim slid down the slope. They were too busy to see him. The woman turned again and ran in the direction of the rock

81

tangle just below Jim. He dropped into a cup thick with brush. Something buzzed dryly, and he smashed down the metal-shod butt of the rifle on the ugly, flat, triangular head of a rattlesnake. The thick, powerful body wound itself about his left leg.

Another man came from the house, staggering a little in his drunkenness and eagerness as he ran toward the desperate woman. Her great dark eyes saw the face in the brush.

"Bandidos!" she screamed.

There was no time for Jim to deliberate now. He'd have to take her word for it. In any case they meant little good toward the naked woman, and the two bodies mutely testified to their profession.

Jim fired once. The two men who stood together dashed back into the brush. The man at the spring raised a rifle. Jim fired twice. The Mexican was slammed back over the rocks and his rifle exploded as he fell, sending a whining slug up into the blue. The rifle shot echoes thundered against the hill slopes and ran along the mountain face to die in the distance, but they were closely pursued by others.

Jim hurdled the rocks at his feet, pushing the screaming woman back into the brush. The writhing snake tripped him. He fell headlong, thrusting forward his rifle as he did so, and the snake saved his life, for slashing lead cut the air where Jim had been standing. He rolled over and fired into the brush where the pair of bandits had vanished, aiming at the gun flashes and puffs of smoke. A man screamed and fell thrashing down the slope, rolling over and over until he fell from a low cliff to crash into the thick brush below.

A bullet smashed into Jim's right boot heel, tearing it off, numbing his lower leg. Another plucked his hat from his head. He fired into the brush again. The Mexican stood up and fired at a fifty-foot range. Jim grunted as the slug smashed into his left shoulder. He fired a round from the rifle with his right hand and then dropped the weapon. He swayed up to his feet, pulling free his Colt. Three times the six-shooter slammed back into his hand, and the Mexican fell backward in death, dropping his smoking rifle.

The big gringo swayed on his feet, his eyes wide with shock. The hot blood ran down inside his shirt and undershirt. He turned slowly to look at the remaining bandit. The Colt fell from Jim's hand.

The Mexican stood there, head and shoulders bent forward, looking at Jim with his one eye, for the other was a puckered hole in his seamed brown face. The Mexican slowly sheathed his nickel-plated pistol and swiftly drew his *saca tripas*. This gringo would have to be gutted like a chicken for what he had done. No easy, swift death for him.

The woman screamed again, the echoes flying down the now strangely quiet hillside.

The Mexican tested the razor edge of his curved knife with his thumb. He walked slowly toward Jim, his one eye like an amber marble, unblinking as the stare of a basilisk. He faded in and out of Jim's sight like a chimera.

The Mexican was within ten feet of Jim when Jim went down, clawing at his belly with both hands in what seemed to be intense pain. The Mexican laughed. He closed in and thrust down with the knife.

The silver-mounted derringer in Jim's right hand spat flame and smoke. The soft-nosed .41 slug caught the Mexican low in the guts. As he fell he drove the knife at Jim's contorted face, and the razor edge ripped across Jim's right cheek to match the scar on the other side. Jim fired the second barrel of the stingy gun. The slug smashed into the bandit's mouth and up into his brain. He fell heavily across Jim.

Then it was very quiet. Jim lay with his blood-masked face against the harsh ground. His left arm and shoulder were completely numbed. The waves of excruciating pain would come after the shock of the impact died away. Slowly he raised his right hand to his slashed face, and he winced as he felt the torn lips of the wound.

The bandit's body was rolled off him. Jim turned his face upward to look at the woman. She was still naked. Her eyes were wide in fear and compassion for the big gringo who had come out of nowhere to save her from multiple rape and possible murder. She was not young, but not very old either, and her body was that of a much younger woman, firm-fleshed and luscious. Jim closed his eyes. Waves of faintness swept over him. He felt his face strike the ground once more.

The last thing he remembered was soft hands working on him, ripping away shirt and undershirt, stanching the big hole in his shoulder, washing the wound in his face and binding it, and all the time she worked on him he was acutely conscious that her warm, full breasts touched him constantly, and once his hand touched the velvet smoothness of a full thigh. After that there was nothing but limbo.

Chapter Ten

He came out of the fever very slowly. There were times when he was aware of movements, voices, actions, and then he would drift off into that vague, hazy land where nothing was ever very clear, and where, at times, he was sure he was dreaming. But gradually he grew aware of other things. Of deft, sure hands bathing him and shaving him. Of soft flesh pressing against him as he was moved about. Once he opened his eyes to see a thick tress of dark hair just above his face, and the faint fragrance of perfume mingled with that of warm, feminine flesh came to him, and then he was gone again.

He opened his eyes one day and did not move. Above him was a corbeled, whitewashed ceiling. He moved only his eyes. To his right were two deep-set windows, and through them came sunlight, shifting as though it came through the moving branches of trees. In one corner was a neat beehive fireplace. A massive chest of drawers stood against a wall, and a crucifix hung above it. There were several wall niches with Indian-faced *santos* within them. The bed in which he lay was massive also. He looked down at his arms lying atop the neat spread, and at his hands. He was stunned as he saw his hands. Once strong and brown, they were now white and lifeless looking, and the hairs seemed to stand alone, like the charred trunks of trees left when fire has swept a mesa.

Birds twittered beyond the windows. He heard the faint braying of a burro. The wind shifted, and an unseen windmill began to hum its busy song. Then clearest of all came the heady, pleasing laughter of children at play.

He closed his eyes. Weakness filled his limbs, and for a moment he thought he was going to drift off into limbo again, but by a conscious effort of his will he held himself in the land of the living. Memories came slowly back to him, piece by puzzling piece, and he fitted them together like a child, by patient trial and error. There had been a day of hazy sunshine. No, it had been late afternoon, closing swiftly

onto dusk. There had been the smoke of a campfire. No, a
house. No, the house had long been abandoned. Smoke. . . .
Smoke? It had been smoke, but not from a house, but from
a fire where clothing, leather, and flesh had burned in an
acrid, sweetish-smelling combination. For a long time he lay
thinking. There had been some shooting. He thought hard.
Men had died there in the hazy sunlight and the drifting
smoke of the fire and the gun muzzles. Who had died, and
why?

He slowly dragged his right hand over to his left shoulder
where a dull, nagging ache persisted, like the beginning of an
abscessed tooth. His shoulder was neatly bandaged. He had
been wounded, then. He remembered that. Slowly, like a
snake uncoiling in its den after the sleep of winter, his right
hand touched his chin and then passed up to his right cheek
where something lay on the taut skin like a thick-bodied
worm. His questing fingers touched the hard granulation of a
newly healed wound.

Jim wet his dry lips. His mind drifted again. Again he
drove it back to its task. Then, with startling clarity, he saw
her, naked, screaming, wide-eyed with pain and sheer terror,
running across the ground toward him. "Mother of the
Devil!" he yelled in a hoarse, cracked voice. "The woman!
What happened to the woman?"

Soft footfalls sounded outside the room, and the thick
door swung back on gently creaking hinges. She stood there
framed in the wide doorway, dark, thick hair plaited in a
heavy coil which crossed a smooth white shoulder exposed
by the low, wide neck of the white blouse she wore, and
rested high on a full breast, like a kitten asleep. Her full
skirt fell from her smoothly rounded hips, and beneath the
embroidered edge of the skirt he saw the tiniest of feet, bare
except for huaraches. It was her eyes that held him fascinated.
Like those of a fawn, but full of a compassion and a life no
fawn had ever exhibited.

She crossed herself. *"Con el favor de Dios,"* she said in
a soft, almost husky voice. "With the favor of God you are
with us again, Senor Murdock."

She came beside the bed and placed a soft, smooth little
hand on his forehead. She smiled. "Yes," she said with de-
light. "Everyone will be so pleased."

He looked up at her, wincing a little as the muscles drew
in his shoulder. "You know who I am," he said. "Who are
you?"

"You do not remember?"

He narrowed his eyes. "The woman at the spring!" he said. "Yes! I remember now."

She reddened and looked away. "I am Rafaela Velarde," she said.

"Your servant, Señorita Velarde," he said.

She straightened the spread. "Señora Velarde," she corrected him.

"I am sorry for that, senora," he said with a smile.

"You Americans," she said with a flirt of her lovely head.

He looked about the room. "How long have I been here?"

She tilted her head to one side and counted on the tips of her slim fingers. "Five, no six!" she said.

He eyed her narrowly. "Days?"

"*Weeks*, Senor Murdock."

He closed his eyes again. It was impossible.

"The doctor said the bullet might have been poisoned."

"There was much fever, then?"

She placed her hand on his forehead again, and he looked up at her. "It was very close," she said quietly. "The doctor said you had the strength of a dozen men and the stubbornness of a mule."

Jim smiled. "I think he knows me pretty well."

"Would you like a mirror?"

"Yes, please."

She brought it to him and held it in front of his face. A stranger stared back at him with deep-set gray eyes. A gaunt death's-head of a face. A thin white scar traced a course down his hollow left cheek, and on the other cheek was a twisted reddish scar. He shook his head. "He did a neat job," he said.

She took away the mirror. "When you have strength you will feel and look better. I will get some soup." She placed the mirror on the wardrobe and walked to the door, gently swaying hips intriguing Jim. He *must* be recovering.

"Where am I?" he asked.

She turned and smiled. "San Federico," she said, and then she was gone, closing the door behind her.

The children laughed again. The mule brayed. The windmill hummed on and on.

"San Federico?" said Jim. He shook his head. *"San Federico?"* He rested his head on the pillow. "Well, I'll be double-dipped in a vat of fresh manure!"

He shifted in the bed, and slowly worked himself up into a semi-sitting position. "Rafaela," he said softly. He remembered all too clearly now. He remembered that lush body, exposed to the hot, lusting eyes of those two-legged animals at the spring. He remembered, too, when she had come to him to help him, forgetting her nakedness in her efforts to stanch his wounds. He might very well have died except for her. "Six weeks," he whispered. He shook his head. With all his months of searching he had not found San Federico, only to find it by sheer luck. The hard way, he thought.

The sun had gone when she returned with a tray. She lighted candles as Jim watched her. Everything she did she did with an effortless grace. He ate slowly as she busied herself about the room. "I have been looking for San Federico for a long time," he said.

"It has been here a long time," she said.

He finished his soup and leaned back against a pillow. She rolled a cigarette for him and placed it between his lips, then lighted it, leaning close, so close that he did not dare look down, for he knew that her blouse would be hanging free from her body. She straightened up and rolled herself a cigarette. She lighted it and blew a puff of smoke.

"There was a Colonia Federico beyond the mountains," he said at last. "I was told the people who had lived there had left that place because of a curse and had come beyond the Sierra Vallecillos to make a new home, a place to be called San Federico. That was all I knew. Strange that I have spent so many weeks on the trail in Sonora, and yet no one knew of this place. Not a word from anyone. Not a trace, and then to find it this way, or rather, to have it find me."

She studied him closely. "Did you not think of looking elsewhere for San Federico?"

"No," he said. "Beyond the Sierra Vallecillos. That was what I was told. But no one knew for sure."

She took the cigarette from her full lips. "It is very simple," she said. "You are not in Sonora, Senor Murdock, but in Arizona Territory, in your United States of America." She laughed at the surprised look on his face. "The people of Colonia Federico did come west of the Sierra Vallecillos to find a new home. It was too wild, too dangerous, because of the Apaches and Yaquis. The people scattered. Some of them drifted west to Hermosillo and Guaymas, or into the mining country. My husband and I came to Arizona for better medical care because of his wounds, and because he had a cousin who was an American citizen. My husband died."

There was a flicker of interest in Jim's eyes.

She ground out the cigarette butt in a dish and looked sideways at him. "He was my first husband," she said quietly. "I married his cousin a year ago. Senor Velarde. The owner

87

of Rancho San Federico. I think you must already know the name of my first husband."

He narrowed his brows and stared uncomprehendingly at her.

"He was Teniente Teodoro Abeyta," she said. "The hero of Colonia Federico."

"How did you know I knew about him?"

She shrugged. "We were on our way here when the bandits struck. I did not know who you were when I had you brought here, north of the border. It was necessary, you understand, to identify you. We looked through your things. I found a picture of myself taken some years ago with my two children. There was a watch, too. I knew it well. It had been presented to my husband for his heroism at Colonia Federico. I have not seen that watch for many years. Where did you get it?"

Jim rolled another cigarette and lighted it. He eyed her through the thin cloud of smoke that drifted toward the open window. How much did she know? Was it possible that she knew Orlando Abeyta had died a felon's death far north of Rancho San Federico?

"There was some question about you having the watch," she added. "But, for what you did at the spring, we forgave anything else."

"I did not steal it," he said.

"I never believed that you did," she said. She sat down on the edge of the bed and studied him closely with those lovely eyes of hers. Something else came back to Jim. Something the priest had said about Orlando Abeyta. *He once told me he would never marry. Orlando Abeyta was in love when he was very young, but it was an unrequited love.* A piece of the puzzle slipped suddenly into place. Rafaela was older than Orlando would have been, perhaps not by very much, but these Mexican women married very young. A coward, a boy who had wanted to be a priest, sensitive and proud, who had become a soldier, not by choice, perhaps because he had deeply loved the woman who had married his elder brother, an officer and a hero.

"Where is he?" she asked softly.

Jim looked at the tip of his cigarette.

"Is he dead?"

Jim nodded.

"He was a friend of yours? Is that why you came to find us?"

Jim looked at her. "He was not my friend," he said. Could he tell her how Orlando had died?

She stood up and paced back and forth. "Something terrible happened to him," she said. "I know."

The wind had shifted. It blew in through the window. The candles guttered and flared, casting her shadow on the white-washed wall. She stopped pacing and looked directly at Jim. "How did he die? Why have you come here to tell us?"

Jim fingered his new face scar. "Who was the coward of Colonia Federico?" he countered.

"How did you know about that?"

He shrugged. "I know," he said quietly. He looked up at her. "It was Orlando, wasn't it?"

"It was not his fault! He was no coward. There are many kinds of cowards. In his own way he was a brave man. It was a label they placed on him."

"Why did they do it?" he asked.

She wet her full lips and looked away. "It was after the fight. There were many wounded. The ground was stained with blood. Men were screaming in their pain. There was no doctor at Colonia Federico." Her voice died away.

"Go on," he said gently.

She caught her breath. "There were only a few soldiers left standing on their feet. My husband was badly wounded. He was wounded, but he was an officer and a soldier of Mexico. He gave orders to kill the enemy wounded. It was the custom. There was never any quarter given or asked for in that type of warfare. You understand?"

Jim nodded. "I have experienced such warfare," he said.

"Orlando was thought to have been killed or wounded. It was not so. He had hidden himself away so that he would not kill. My husband found out about it. In front of the people of Colonia Federico and the few soldiers left alive he gave Orlando a direct order to kill the enemy wounded. Orlando must do it alone to redeem himself." She laughed bitterly.

"He did not do it?" asked Jim.

She shook her head. "It was not within that gentle boy to kill like that, or any other way. . . ."

"I can guess what happened to him," he said.

She nodded. "They shaved his head, stripped his buttons from him, and drummed him from the ranks."

"Because he could not kill."

"Yes," she said. She took the makings and rolled a cigarette. She looked at Jim over the flare of the match. "How did he die?"

"Bravely."

"But why?" she said.

He could at least tell a little lie. "There was a gunfight. A man was killed. It was thought that Orlando had killed this man. His friends shot down Orlando. Before he died he gave me those things you found."

She walked to the window and turned her back toward Jim. Her lovely shoulders shook a little. "Was there anything he said?" she asked.

The wind seemed to die away and it was very quiet, as though the oncoming night too wanted to hear what Jim Murdock had to say.

"Rafaela," said Jim. "That was what he said."

"There are many women named Rafaela," she said huskily.

"Perhaps. But that is what he said."

Her shoulders drooped a little. "It was I who gave him the watch," she said, without turning.

"A little cruelty, perhaps?"

She shook her head. "He wanted it."

"And the picture?"

"I did not know he had it."

Jim wet his dry lips. This was more painful than his healing wounds.

She turned slowly. "Would you like to see the children?" she said.

"Very much. Your husband as well."

She took the tray and walked to the door, looking back over her shoulder at him. "He is in Tucson on business," she said. "He will not be back for at least a week. Two days ago a package came from him for you. Medicines. Don Federico Velarde, my husband, is a fine man, and a good stepfather to my children."

"Federico again?" His eyes held hers. *He will be gone at least a week,* thought Jim.

She nodded. "There was a *cura* here at one time, many years ago, long before the Americans took Arizona from my people. This was a holy place, but it fell upon evil times. My husband's grandfather took it over and named this place after his patron saint, Saint Federico. After that, each eldest son has taken that name. You must rest now."

The door closed behind her. Jim slowly fashioned another cigarette. There was something in the woman that cried out to him, but why he did not know. She had been married twice, and surely both husbands had been good to her, and she had probably loved Teodoro. Jim wet the end of the paper and thumbed the paper together. He snapped a match on his thumbnail and lighted the cigarette. But she had been loved by the ill-fated Orlando and she had wanted

90

to know his last words. Had she loved him too? What kind of woman was this? He closed his eyes. *"Don Federico Velarde, my husband, is a fine man, and a good stepfather to my children."* He opened his eyes and blew a smoke ring. "He will not be back for at least a week," he said aloud.

The wind shifted. A shutter banged. A draft of air swirled in through the open windows and played with the guttering candles.

Jim felt his wounded shoulder. It would be some time before he could ride. Until that time he would be a guest in the casa of Don Federico Velarde.

The door opened and Rafaela brought in her two children. There was Teodoro, a grave-faced faced boy of perhaps twelve, and little Teresa, perhaps seven or eight years of age. Teresa was formed from the same pattern as her mother, with mischievous eyes and a flirtatious look. Teodoro? Once, the boy looked quickly sideways at Jim, and for an instant, the blinking of an eye, perhaps, Jim thought he saw the face of Orlando Abeyta.

When they were gone, Jim lay there for a long time staring up at the dim ceiling. He had to leave this place. He had done what he had set out to do. He had told Orlando's kin of his death. He had found out what kind of man Orlando Abeyta had been. It had taken many months. It would soon be time for him to ride north, back to his own country, to find Three Forks and a girl named Jessica. Then it would all be over, and he'd be able to sleep well once again, and the dog would be off his back. So far it had not been an easy task, nor were his problems over. He dropped off to sleep, and as he did so the oval face of Rafaela appeared to him, and there were other things as well. Things that disturbed his sleep as it had not been disturbed for many months.

The sixth day after Jim's return to the world of the living he had spent outside in the bright sunshine of late summer, watching the children at play, looking at the purple haze over the hills, listening to the distant bawling of the cattle, and also to the voice of Rafaela as she gave orders to her servants. The doctor had visited Jim twice in that time. All Jim needed now was rest and good food. The doctor had done all he could do. The doctor, and Rafaela, thought Jim. *Rafaela.* She was rarely out of his mind.

That night they dined together in the huge, low-ceilinged dining room of the sprawling hacienda, after the children had gone to bed, and if Rafaela Velarde had not known she had made a conquest prior to that dinner, she must surely have known it then.

They sat together a long time in the moonlight of the patio, talking of Orlando and of Teodoro, of Colonia Federico, which was well remembered by Rafaela. She remembered, too, the old padre who had given Jim his first real lead in his search for the kin of Orlando Abeyta.

Later, in his room, with the dying moonlight silvering patches of the polished floor, Jim paced back and forth, smoking, his arm in a sling to ease his shoulder, thinking of Rafaela until he thought he must be going mad.

It took a long time for him to sleep. He did not know when he dropped off, but the scene that came before him in his sleep occurred some hours before the coming of the dawn. He saw those damned trees of hell standing on the cold, windswept ridge. He saw the bitter fruit of men's sudden madness swinging like grisly pendulums in the eerie grip of the whining wind, and he shouted aloud in his terror.

He opened his eyes to feel the icy sweat covering his naked flesh, and his body shook like aspen leaves. He closed his eyes and turned his head desperately from side to side to shake the awful dregs of the nightmare from his mind. The room was pitch-dark when he opened his eyes. Then the door swung open to reveal Rafaela standing there in her thin gown, a candle in her hand and fear upon her lovely face. Fear, not for herself, but for Jim Murdock. She came quickly to him and sat on the edge of the bed, holding the candle in her free hand as she stroked his wet brow. He slid his right arm about her slender waist and looked up at her face. For a long, long moment they looked into each other's eyes, forgetting why he had cried out and why she had come. She bent close to him. The candle fell to the floor and extinguished itself, and she was in his arms, lips pressing hotly against his mouth while his free hand roved her soft, warm body.

Now was the time. There was nothing, no one, to hold them back from each other, from what both of them had known in their own minds for days. They were on the very edge of complete surrender to each other. Then they seemed suspended, balanced in time, as though it were really non-existent, and a moment later her hot lips parted from his and she drew back her long dark hair from his face and naked chest. His right arm fell away from her. Slowly she sat up and pulled her filmy gown about her shoulders. Another moment or two drifted slowly past. A cold, searching

92

wind crept in through the windows and chilled the two of them.

"Good night, Jaime," she whispered.

"Good night, Rafaela," he said huskily.

She walked slowly to the door, half expecting him to call her back and knowing she could not refuse him, while he wanted to call her back and knew in full conscience that he could not.

"I am leaving in the morning," he said at last.

She nodded her head and then closed the door behind her.

He lay there for a long time until the inner fires waned and then sank into a dim glow, leaving a thick layer of ashes on the deep-seated passion within him. There seemed no longer a great haste to leave the rancho and travel north on the last part of his self-imposed mission. As he had left a part of himself on the grim gallows hill back in Ute Crossing that cold morning when three men had been lynched, so he had also left a part of himself when old Augustin Galeras had died in the Sierra Vallecillos. The deaths of Lyss, Slim, Jules, and the four *bandidos* meant nothing to Jim, for he had killed in such fashion before, but the deaths of the others had affected him deeply.

Something was driving him on and on. Perhaps he was seeking himself. Loneliness had become part and parcel of his life. Perhaps he needed someone to share his thoughts and plans. It might be that this was assuming far more importance in his mind than it merited, but what else was there for a man to do in an effort to achieve wholeness?

He knew there was deadly danger for him up north. Lyss had died in a muddy alley in Las Cruces and Slim and Jules had died near Colonia Federico for some deep, dark reason that had something to do with the hanging of those three men in Ute Crossing. Someone wanted Jim Murdock permanently out of the way. Perhaps they had lost track of him, thought him dead in the Sierra Madre. It would be easy to stay in the south and avoid the prospect of sudden, violent death if he returned north.

He opened his eyes and stared at the dim ceiling. "Jessica," he said. He knew he had to go.

Chapter Eleven

The summer was dying as the tall, gaunt man, his set face marked for life with two scars, rode slowly north from the border country, gathering his strength as he rode, camping out at times in the lonely canyons beside chuckling streams, lingering there for days, only to saddle up and ride on again. Patagonia saw him, and Sonoita, and he lingered for days in brawling Tombstone, quietly walking the streets of the toughest town in the West. He bothered no one and no one bothered him. They knew the stamp and quality of his breed. Such men were better left alone. His drift took him north to Benson, and then by train to Lordsburg, in New Mexico Territory. He dallied for a time in Silver City, finding the food passable, the liquor good, his luck at the tables better than it had ever been, and the company of a little, dark-eyed Cajun girl gradually dulled the sharp edge of his memories of Rafaela Velarde.

In Albuquerque an ex-army surgeon he had known along the border inspected his shoulder and pronounced it well again. The hollows had filled out in his face and the sun, wind, rain, and good air had made him seem like the old Jim Murdock. The real wounds were invisible.

It was easy, far too easy, to try to avoid the inevitable. He turned away from the valley of the Rio Grande at Bernalillo and rode northwesterly at a steady pace for days through the lonely, windswept country until he reached the San Juan. It occurred to him only then that he was really heading for Meadows to see a little man in a derby hat who bought and sold anything and everything. Fella by the name of Sam. *"You will stop by on your way back, maybe? It was a pleasure doing business with you."* Jim grinned.

The leaves had turned when he reached Meadows. The country was a glory of scarlet, purple, and gold, with a haziness always in the distance. He could see the wolf-fanged mountains to the north that held Ute Crossing in their grasp, and the highest peak of them all, Warrior Peak, was just visible, tipped with a golden cap from the rays of the sinking sun. He was getting close to home, if one could still call it that.

Meadows dozed in the bright, clear sunlight. The air had a thin and brittle quality to it. The cottonwoods along the street were like yellow flames. A blacksmith's hammer beat a steady, metallic song that echoed against the low hills just beyond the town.

Jim dismounted and tethered the dun. He slapped the dust from his trail clothing. The building where Sam held forth in solitary splendor seemed to lean just a little more from the perpendicular. Jim opened the door. The bell tinkled rustily. He walked slowly between the piles of dusty boxes, a vast mausoleum of the unused and useless, waiting for someone who might, just *might*, mind you, have use for them. Their hope was as dead as the dusty air of the gloomy cavern in which they waited.

The bell stopped tinkling.

"You are wanting to buy or sell, maybe?" a soft voice asked out of nowhere, like a disembodied spirit trying to establish contact with the world of the living. A derby hat seemed to rise by itself from behind a rampart of dusty feed sacks.

"Hello, Sam," said Jim.

Sam studied Jim. "Mr. Murdock," he said quietly. "It has been a long time. You have changed."

Jim instinctively touched the scar on his right cheek.

Sam held up a hand. "No, it is not that. Not that alone, my friend. It is something else. I cannot put my hand on it."

Jim nodded. "I know what you mean," he said.

"The drinks are on you, stranger!" shrieked the parrot.

Jim grinned. He took out his cigar case and opened it, holding it out to Sam. "I know," said Jim. "You came west from Pittsburg because you had a cough. You should smoke? Crazy you'd be!"

Sam smiled. "It is good to see you in such a mood," he said. "It has not been easy for you. Tell me! You found, maybe, the woman Sarah?"

Jim nodded. "I left her the money you gave me, Sam."

"Good!" Sam tilted his head to one side. "You want to talk, maybe, about it?"

Jim shook his head.

"You found, maybe, the others you were looking for?"

"I didn't say I was looking for any others."

"You didn't have to, Jim."

"I found the kin of the Mexican who was hanged."

"But the kin of the boy, you did not find them?"

95

"That is why I came back, Sam." Jim bit the end from a cigar and held a match to the tip.

Sam rubbed his cheek. "Maybe you should have stayed down south."

"Why?"

"After you left for the south there was a man who came looking for you. A big man. Such a nose he had! A big, thick moustache. Eyebrows like raveled rope above his eyes. a mean-looking character, Jim. I was afraid from him. I told him you had gone to Albuquerque. But nothing more, Jim! I swear!"

Jim blew out the match. "He won't be coming back," he said quietly.

Sam shivered. "There were two more men some time after he was gone."

"One of them tall and slim with sandy hair? The other dark, very dark, broad-shouldered, and had a slight limp? Names of Jules and Slim?"

Sam smiled weakly. "They won't be back either?"

"No." Jim blew a smoke ring. "Were there any others?"

"None that I saw or talked to, Jim. But I heard there was two men here a month or so after the second two left. They hung around drinking and then went south."

"Any names?"

"One of them was called Barney. The other I do not know. Like I said, Jim, I didn't see them or talk to them, and I didn't want to. But there is something else, my friend. Something you should know. About your brother."

Jim took the cigar from his mouth. "Ben?"

"Yes. You did not know?"

"Know what?" asked Jim quietly.

Sam looked away. He took off his faded derby and turned the brim around and around in his thin hands. "It is a terrible thing to tell a friend," said Sam softly.

"Tell me, Sam," said Jim in a harsh voice.

Sam looked directly at Jim. "He is dead, my friend."

"How did he die?"

"It was not long after you left. We heard the story here in little bits and pieces. It was said he drove his buggy very fast."

"He did," agreed Jim.

"They found the team still drawing the front wheels. They searched back along the road. The rest of the buggy they found in the creek near his house." Sam stopped and wet his dry lips. He swallowed. "Your brother was a cripple? No?"

Jim nodded. He could plainly see Warrior Creek and the

black water against the newly fallen snow as he had last seen it. The creek wasn't deep but it ran very fast, and the water would be icy cold.

Sam rubbed his thin throat. "They found him in the spring. Very strange, too, for his body was found on the bank on the ranch that used to belong to your family, Jim. Like maybe he had come home. No one knew where you were."

It was very quiet in the big store. Even the parrot had stopped rustling, preening, and squawking in his cage.

Jim shook his head. "He was a man of principle, Sam. A man who fought for justice. It was almost an obsession with him."

"Such things are not obsessions," said the little man. "If they are, then more of us should maybe be obsessed." He eyed Jim. "He was, maybe, the only one of your family left?"

"Yes."

"It is a lonely thing for a man to have no family. I know."

Jim relighted his cigar. It wasn't in him to accept sympathy. Much as he might want it, he always avoided it. To him it was a mark of weakness, and yet he knew not why he felt that way. He was like a lobo or a wild dog who would crawl away to lick his own wounds without benefit of sympathy. Would it be that way the rest of his life?

"You are going north again?" asked Sam.

"Yes."

Sam shrugged. "You are like a man who courts death."

"There are things a man has to do."

"He does not have to seek his own self-destruction."

"You talk like a preacher."

Sam smiled. "A rabbi! You will stay a few days? There is room here for you."

"Here?"

"Come and see."

Sam led the way into the back of the immensely long store. He opened a door and ushered Jim into a surprising room. Books lined two of the walls. A polished piano stood against one wall. Pictures graced the walls here and there. A fine Navajo rug was on the floor.

"You surprise me, Sam," said Jim.

"This is my hideout, Jim. Days I spend in the front. Nights and Sundays here, reading my good friends the books."

"You have no real friends here, Sam?"

Sam shook his head. He glanced sideways at Jim. "I have been waiting. Maybe I have found such a friend."

Jim blew a ring of smoke and punched a lean finger

through it. "A gunman? A killer? Me? Not me, Sam. I'm not your style."

Sam busied himself with a dusty wine bottle. "Not the guns and the killings, Jim. It is something else. We make a strange pair, but we are friends, and you know it."

Jim nodded.

Sam filled two glasses and handed one to Jim. "While you are here, stay with me, Jim. I know you have to go. Maybe if I was in your boots I would do the same thing. Who is to say?"

They touched the glasses together. The wine was delicious. In a little while the two of them began to talk of many things, far removed from violent death and dusty merchandise, and when the dusk came, and Sam locked up the store and turned to the big range in his kitchen to fashion a meal, Jim knew that the little man was right. Sam had found a friend.

When Jim left his new friend, Sam came to the door of the store with him. "You will maybe let me know how you make out?" he asked.

Jim checked his saddle girth. "If I can't, someone else will," he said dryly.

"Do not talk like that, my friend. Find this Jessica. Tell her of her brother."

"She likely already knows the story, Sam."

"Even so, she would like to hear it, maybe, from a man who has spent so many months of his time to tell the kin of those three unfortunate men."

Jim turned and stuck out a big hand. Sam gripped it. "When this is all over and you are at peace," said Sam, "what do you plan to do?"

"Get a little ranch. Hunt and fish. Read a few books."

"You will do this alone?"

"Probably."

Sam hesitated. "When I first met you I said a partner I didn't need. Maybe, when you look for this ranch, you could use some cash. A partner, maybe?"

"You, Sam?"

Sam nodded. He looked back at the leaning building. "Of this place I am sick."

"I'll consider the offer, Sam."

Sam turned. "Maybe I could be a Yiddisher cowboy, hey?"

Jim grinned as he mounted. "Adios, Sam." He rode west along the wide street, then turned in his saddle. "Hey, Sam!" he called out. "If we have a Yiddisher cowboy we'd have to have kosher cows!"

The little man was still laughing when Jim turned off from the street and took the road north out of Meadows. The smile vanished from Sam's face. He opened the door and walked inside. The bell tinkled. "Shut up!" snapped Sam at the bell.

"The drinks are on you, stranger!" squawked the parrot. "You too!" shouted Sam. He vanished into his hideout.

For a man carrying a message of death, and wondering in the back of his mind what further violence lay in store for him, there was deep enjoyment in Jim Murdock as he worked his way through the mountain approaches that bright morning. He was going home, for better or for worse. It had been a long time. A long, dusty, deadly trail from Ute Crossing to Las Cruces, Chihuahua City, Colonia Federico, and Rancho San Federico, and now he was nearing the end.

A fine, needlelike drizzle was falling on the valley, slanting down from the great range of mountains to the east, drifting across the thick timber at the bases of the heights, and stippling the leaden surface of the river. The rain had darkened the false-fronted wooden buildings of the town and was puddling in the hollows and ruts of the road. Hipshot horses stood patiently at the racks in front of the stores and the saloons, mostly the saloons. The harder rains, the gully washers and fence lifters, would come later, forecasting the bitter winter. It was getting along toward that time.

A chain of sheet lightning zigzagged across the streaming sky and forked into a bluff. A low rumble of drums came from the thunder gods. The rain came down harder and harder until the bluffs were hidden from sight.

A lone horseman crossed the wooden bridge that spanned the rushing river, hunched into his slicker collar, hat pulled low over his eyes, a tiny spark of flame showing from the cigarette he cupped in his hand. He looked at the high, warped front of a store. "Three Forks General Mercantile Company," he read. Jim kneed the horse toward the nearest rack and swung down into the thick mud. He unstrapped a poncho from the cantle and hung it over the horse. He stepped up onto the sagging wooden sidewalk and found himself looking directly at a dirty-windowed saloon. "Well, fancy that," he said with a tired smile. It had been a three-day ride through the mountains.

He walked into the saloon and rested an elbow on the end of the bar. The bar was pretty well lined. Four men played poker at a rear table. A swamper was listlessly mopping up

99

the water from a leak in the roof. There wasn't much talking. It wasn't talking weather. Just drinking weather.

"Rye," said Jim to the bartender.

Bottle and glass were placed in front of Jim. The bartender was a melancholy-looking soul with an uneasy Adam's apple. One of his eyes, slightly larger than the other, seemed to wander off on a mission of its own now and then, to be brought back only by a conscious effort. "Long ride?" said the bar critter.

"Passable," said Jim. He filled the glass.

"From the north?"

"South."

No one looked at Jim. Saddle tramps were a dime a dozen in the Three Forks country.

"Looking for work?" said the bar critter.

Jim tossed down the drink. "Not exactly," he said.

The man wiped the zinc-topped bar. "Well, you are or you ain't," he said. "Temple Smeed is looking for teamsters."

"Out of my line," said Jim. He felt the rye hit his cold guts and explode. His face suddenly felt warm.

"Buck Witty is looking for riders."

Jim eyed the man. "You run the employment agency here?" he asked with a smile.

"No. Sort of a hobby of mine, mister." The sad eyes studied Jim and the two scars, the hard set of the jaw, the gray eyes that seemed to make a man a little too uncomfortable to stare at very long. He had known all along that this wasn't any teamster or line rider. No, and not a livery hand, and certainly not a townsman. Gambler? No. Gunfighter. . . .

Jim refilled the glass. "I'm looking for a girl named Jessica," he said quietly.

A broad-shouldered, bearded man laughed. "Hell!" he said explosively. "Who ain't?"

Jim looked at him. "You know her?" he asked.

"No."

"I wasn't talking to you, mister," said Jim evenly.

Hard dark eyes peered into Jim's eyes, and what the bearded man saw he did not like. "Sorry," he said. "I thought it was funny at the time. No offense, mister."

"Forget it," said Jim. "Pour yourself a drink."

The man nodded. He wanted no part of this lobo.

The bartender leaned on the bar. "Girl by the name of Jessica lives up the North Fork," he said. "Jessica Lyle. Lives by herself except for one hand." He grinned. "She shoots as good as any man too, mister."

"Lives alone? No people?"

The bartender shrugged. "She had a brother named Jesse. They was twins. No, there ain't no one out there but her and old Jonas."

Jim downed his second drink. The cold was leaving his body. "What happened to her brother?"

The bartender rubbed industriously at an imaginary spot on the zinc while his wandering eye moved back and forth. "What do you want to know for?" he asked quietly.

A gray-faced man halfway up the bar looked at Jim. "Tell him, Les," he said. "Go on. Tell him. I'd like to see the look on his face."

The saloon was suddenly very quiet. The poker players were watching Jim. The swamper was leaning on his mop handle doing the same thing. Every man at the bar except a drunken fool at the end was looking at Jim. The drunk was looking into his empty whiskey glass. It was all that really seemed to interest him.

Les took a final swipe at the imaginary spot. He looked directly at Jim, and for once his loose eye was steady. "The kid was lynched over to Ute Crossing a little less than a year ago," he said. "Lynched for murder."

There was no expression on Jim's face. "I know," he said.

The gray-faced man's hand tightened about his shot glass. "No one bothered to tell the girl," he said bitterly. "No one told her until the whole damned town knew about it from the Denver newspapers. It was too late then to remember she got delivery of the same newspaper. Someone should have broken the news to her before that."

"Take it easy, Kyle," said the bartender.

"The sons of bitches," said Kyle. "That kid never killed no one. His sister has more guts in her little finger than he had in his whole body. There was only the two of them, and some of the bastards around here used to chase after Jessica, and the kid couldn't do anything about it. They drove that boy outa here."

Les rubbed his thin throat. "Well, anyways, there ain't no one bothers her now," he said.

A short, red-faced man nodded. "Beats the hell outa me how she keeps that place a-goin'," he said. "My missus told me to go over and give her a hand. She says to me: 'No thanks, Mr. Watts, I kin take care of myself and my property.' I felt like a damned jackass about it. She don't want nothin' to do with nobody, I tell you."

101

"Cute trick, too," said a grinning cowpoke. "One time I was hunting strays over on the North Fork. I stops to pass the time of day. Well, maybe I did get too fresh. I crossed the North Fork two jumps and a holler ahead of a .44/40 slug."

The gray-faced man looked at him. "You let her alone, Kelly," he said thinly.

Kelly shoved back his glass. "What for, Kyle? You got a brand on her? She turned you down half a dozen times, from what I hear."

Kyle turned and looked at him. "You got a big mouth, Kelly," he said softly.

Les walked to the middle of the bar. "Drinks on the house," he said. "Sam! Get to leaning on that mop handle! Jerry! Stick some nickels in the piano! You boys at the table want fresh drinks!"

The man named Kyle emptied his glass, wiped his mouth with the back of a hand, and looked at Jim. "What business you got with Jessica Lyle?" he demanded.

"That's my business," said Jim.

Kelly whistled softly. "Now it's you with the big mouth, Kyle," he said.

"Something about her brother?" said Kyle.

Jim emptied his glass and shoved it back. He paid for the drinks. He felt inside his coat for his cigar case, withdrew a long nine, lighted it, and fanned out the match.

"Well?" said Kyle. He stood a little way back from the bar.

Les leaned forward. "One more remark out of you, Kyle," he said quietly, "and I'll cut you off. You know Marshal Craig will back me up. He's had a bellyful of your trouble-making lately."

Kyle wet his lips. He turned back to the bar. He wasn't so damned sure at that that he wanted trouble with the tall, scar-faced man at the end of the bar. There was plenty of time to find out what business he had with Jessica Lyle.

Les looked at Jim. "Cross back over the bridge," he said. "Take the first road to the right. Follow it about five miles to the North Fork. You can't miss it. There's a plank bridge there. The other side of the bridge is Jessica Lyle's property."

"Watch out she don't come a-shootin'!" said Kelly. "Hawwww!"

Jim walked to the door, feeling the eyes of every man in the place, except likely the drunk at the end of the bar, boring a hole into his back.

"You never did tell us your name," said Les.

Jim turned a little. "Murdock," he said. "Jim Murdock." He closed the door behind him.

The drunk slowly raised his head. Just as slowly he looked toward the door. Suddenly it seemed as though he wasn't drunk at all. He paid his tab and put on his slicker. "What time does the company telegraph office close, Les?" he asked.

"Half an hour, Monk."

Monk walked slowly to the door, peered out into the dimness, and saw Jim riding toward the bridge. Monk stepped out onto the boardwalk and hurried up the street toward the telegraph office. It had been a long, long time ago that he had been told to keep an eye out for a tall, scar-faced man named Murdock. Jim Murdock. . . .

Chapter Twelve

The fall rain had thinned out to a misty drizzle when Jim Murdock reached the sagging bridge across the North Fork. Now and then eerie lightning flashes illuminated the dusk and silvered the falling rain. The North Fork was bank-full and already beginning to lap over the rotten planking of the bridge. The structure creaked and groaned in the current. The bloated body of a drowned calf swirled lazily in an eddy on the far side of the stream. There was nothing to be seen beyond the bridge except the dripping woods, dark and secretive, parted by the narrow road, just wide enough for a wagon, which vanished into the dimness. No sign of a house, a cabin, or a shed. Not a sight of an animal or a fence. Nothing but the dark, dripping woods, a rusted mailbox on a tilted post, and the leaden-colored waters of the stream.

Jim rolled a quirly and lighted it, flipping the match into the water. Words came back to him: *"She shoots as good as any man too, mister. . . . That kid never killed no one. His sister has more guts in her little finger than he had in his whole body. . . . She don't want nothin' to do with nobody, I tell you. . . . I crossed the North Fork two jumps and a holler ahead of a .44/40 slug. . . . Watch out she don't come a-shootin'!"*

Jim tapped his side pocket. He could feel the hard lump of the bluish-looking stone within it. It was all he had brought those hundreds of miles and after so many months to give to a girl who had lost her twin brother; likely, according to the barflies in the local saloon, the only near kin she had had around Three Forks.

"By God," said Jim. "What the hell is the matter with me? I didn't come all this distance to be scared of a female gun toter!" He grinned, his saturnine face lighted momentarily by the flare of the cigarette tip as he took a drag. "All the same, I'd rather face a bee-stung she-bear with cubs than a gal wearin' pants and making Winchester music around my ears. You can't shoot back. All you can do is cut stick for the *rio* and hope you reach the brush on the far side ahead of a .44/40 slug, like the man in the saloon said. He was laughing then. He wasn't laughing when she was helping him make up his mind he ought to leave."

He touched the horse with his heels and rode slowly out on the creaking bridge, nervously eyeing that swirling water which had risen higher even as he had watched it. He reached the far side and looked back. "By God," he said. "I won't try that bridge until the North Fork goes down, gun-totin' woman and all!"

The way through the woods was an uneasy way for Jim. Wasn't likely she'd be squatting there in the brush cuddling that damned Winchester of hers, looking for fair game. Not with the rain and the darkness coming on. Still . . .

He had ridden almost a mile and half through the woods when at last he saw them thinning out as the lightning lanced across the sky and struck into a towering, naked butte that dominated the landscape like a brooding giant. He drew rein at the edge of the woods and waited for the next eerie flash. When it came he saw a wide meadowland area stretching beyond the woods, bisected by the road. To the right he thought he caught a glimpse of some cattle bedded down in the edge of the woods. Here and there on the meadowland were outcroppings of lichened rocks, like dislocated bones thrust up against the surface flesh of the earth. The ground at the far end of the open area sloped upward, and the road climbed it and vanished on the far side. There was nothing else to do but traverse that open area, hoping that Jessica Lyle wasn't out prowling with her trusty Winchester.

It was fully dark when he reached the far side. A dilapidated barbed-wire fence stretched on either side of the road, and the remains of a Texas gate had been hauled to one side to clear the road. He rode down the far side of the rise, and then suddenly, when he least expected it, he saw a faint yellowish glow of light beyond a motte of wind-swaying trees. He halted the tired horse and began to roll a cigarette, then thought better of it. A lighted match or the glow of a cigarette could be seen etched against the darkness, giving just enough target and time to slam out a round or two.

He rode slowly forward, then dismounted, and led the dun on. A man on a horse is too big a target. He tethered the dun to a shattered tree, and for a moment his hand lingered on the wet buttstock of his saddle gun, and then he shook his head. A flash of lingering lightning revealed a well-built house of peeled logs, set on a knoll. Light showed from two windows at the side of the house and from one in front. There were other buildings beyond the house. Sheds and a big barn, slightly the worse for wear, a fallen-in log building and a dark-looking structure, likely a bunkhouse. Jim whistled softly. This had been a nice spread at one time.

A dog barked suddenly from an outbuilding. Jim watched the house. The dog barked again and again. Likely he was penned in or chained. The wind shifted and brought the bittersweet odor of woodsmoke to Jim. It brought something else as well, the lovely odor of cooking food. He could have sworn there were fresh-baked rolls or bread, and maybe even a pie or two. He remembered then that he had not eaten all day, except for a few scraps of trail rations around noon.

A dark shape moved near one of the outbuildings. Too low for a man or woman. The dog barked, and Jim knew what the shape was, but it didn't move any closer. He had been right about the animal being chained. Something moved between the light and the window in one of the lighted rooms. The wind brought the sound of a closing door to him. Then he saw someone standing on the edge of the rear porch.

"Hello, the house!" yelled Jim.

The dog slammed against his chain, barking and growling in turns.

Jim walked slowly forward, hands at shoulder level. "You there!" he called out. "I've come to see Miss Lyle on business! Are you Miss Lyle?"

The figure moved. "Not likely," said a man.

"You must be Jonas, then."

"You know a lot about this place, don't you?"

"Damn it! All I know is that Miss Lyle lives here and that

105

my slicker is leaking in this rain! Water running down my sleeves!"

The man laughed. "Then put your hands down, mister! Who are you? What do you want?"

"The name is Murdock! Jim Murdock! I've come to see Miss Lyle." Jim lowered his hands, cursing softly as he felt the water soak the sleeves of his shirt and coat.

Jim waited. He narrowed his eyes. He had the damnedest feeling that someone else was watching him. He saw the man turn his head a little as though someone had spoken to him, and then he nodded. "Bring on your cayuse," said Jonas. "Put him in the barn there. I'll get a lantern."

By the time Jim reached the barn the man was coming from the house with the lantern. He was a short bench-legged man who walked with a slight limp. He grinned at Jim from as homely a face as Jim had ever experienced, but his eyes were squirrel-bright and seemingly friendly. He didn't have on a slicker or a coat, and there was no belt gun at his narrow waist. His face was wrinkled like a dried apple, and it was difficult to tell how old he was, perhaps fifty-five or sixty years of age. His eyes, at least, were still young.

Jim led the dun into the barn. He looked at Jonas. "All right to unsaddle?"

"Why not?"

Jim grinned. "I didn't know what kind of reception I'd get around here."

"Sho! Well, you can't expect a man to go all the way back from where he come from on a night like this."

Jim unsaddled the dun and rubbed him down, covered him with a worn blanket he found in a stall, and fed him. "Times a little hard around here?" he said conversationally as he picked up his saddlebags and cantle roll.

"Not so's you'd notice it. Nice country around here. Good stock. Plenty of water and grazing."

"I noticed that." Jim looked about the cavernous barn. Half a dozen streams of water came down from the roof at the rear of the structure. "Plenty of water. . . ."

"Well, we ain't exactly in business right now."

Jim looked at him. "I heard Miss Lyle would run off anyone in pants."

"She never run me off. 'Course, I'm too damned old to bother much with fillies now. Been a confirmed bachelor all my life, anyways. I never give the name Barlow to no filly. Saves time, money, and trouble, with the accent on trouble." Jonas lifted the lantern from a box. "I sleep in the bunkhouse. Kinda lonely with all them bunks empty there,

106

but I use the foreman's room. There are two bunks in there."

Jim followed the short man through the wet darkness to the sagging bunkhouse. Jonas hung the lantern on a hook in the room. "You can clean up if you like. Supper will be ready in an hour."

Jim nodded. "Does she know I'm here?"

"You joshing? Mister, that gal don't miss a thing." Jonas felt for the makings and rolled a cigarette. He tossed the makings to Jim. "You can start a fire in the stove there and dry out." He lighted the cigarette and fanned out the match. "Where you from, Murdock?"

Jim smiled as he peeled off his slicker, coat, and shirt. "Anywhere and everywhere." He rolled a cigarette and lighted it.

"Colorado man?"

"Originally."

Jonas walked to the door. He looked back. "Ute Crossing, maybe?" he asked quietly.

"I was born in the valley of the Ute."

"Been there lately?"

"Almost a year ago."

The wind shifted and rattled the windowpanes. A cold draft crept through a broken pane and swirled the cigarette smoke about the room.

"Maybe last November, mister?"

Jim looked at the little man. "You're asking a helluva lot of questions, aren't you, mister?"

For a second the bright eyes hardened. "Sorry, Murdock. It really ain't none of my business, is it?"

"You're getting the general idea, Barlow."

Jonas nodded. He closed the door behind him. Jim heard his boots squelch in the mud, and then the sound died away. He heard a door slam.

Jim started a fire and hung his clothing near it. He examined the puckered bullet hole in his shoulder. The cold had made his shoulder a little stiff. He heated water and then washed and shaved. He studied himself in the cracked, gold-flecked mirror. "My God," he breathed. "I look like the devil's twin brother."

He dressed in dry, clean clothing and tied a string tie about his corded neck. He reached for his gun belt and then stopped. He rubbed his jaw. Wasn't exactly polite to walk into a house and sit down to supper carrying a six-gun at your hip. On the other hand, he remembered too well the reputation the young woman had for dealing with men. He satisfied himself with placing his double-barreled derringer in his coat pocket. Maybe the characters in the saloon had been building up a stack about Jessica Lyle, the sharpshooting gal of Three Forks. He grinned. He must have walked into a real setup on that rainy afternoon. He'd be willing to bet they were still laughing into their tanglefoot.

Still, Jessica must know who he was, as Jonas had. Maybe the story of his mission to find the kinfolk of the three dead men had passed through that country. Maybe she was just wondering why it had taken the most part of a year for him to reach Three Forks. He'd have to explain that one. He was sorry for her without even meeting her. He had been sorry for her ever since he had seen the kid die with a hemp necktie cutting off his young life. He was sorrier still that she had learned about his death in clear, cold print in a three-day-old newspaper deposited in that rusty mailbox on the banks of the North Fork.

Jim turned out the lantern and opened the door. The rain was hardly more than a thick mist now. He walked toward the house, the lights warm and cheery through the darkness and mistiness. He stepped up onto the rear porch and flipped away his cigarette. He rapped on the door.

Jonas opened the door. "Almost in time," he said. "Go on in, Murdock. Miss Lyle is waiting for you in the living room." He glanced over his shoulder, then came closer to Jim. "Take it easy on her. She ain't forgot a thing about the kid's death."

Jim wiped his feet and took off his hat. He crossed the brightly lighted kitchen, eyeing a row of fresh-built pies as he did so. The little man, or Jessica, was a prime cook.

He entered the big living room. A fire crackled in the cavernous fieldstone fireplace. A woman, slim as a birch, stood beside the fire, looking down into it. Jim cleared his throat. For a moment she stood there, and then she turned and looked directly at him, and it was like a shade from the other world for the brief span of a second or two, for she was an identical twin, as much as a woman can be twin to a man and not show masculinity, and yet in a way the kid had been more feminine in his appearance. He remembered all too well the sick, ghastly look on the boy's face before he had died. He remembered as well the set blue face of the boy when Jim had cut him down.

"Mr. Murdock," she said quietly. Her voice was much like her brother's had been, as Jim could recall, but there was a firmness in it, a resolution, that the kid had lacked. But then, maybe most any man would have lacked resolution and firmness if he knew he had only minutes before he was to be lynched.

"Miss Lyle," said Jim. He bent his head.

"Jonas said you came from Ute Crossing."

She knew where Jim came from, and it hadn't been Jonas who had told her. This much Jim knew. "I was born in the valley of the Ute," he said quietly. "I returned there almost a year ago after an absence of seven years. I spent only a short time there before leaving for New Mexico and Mexico."

There was a long pause. Jim narrowed his eyes. His impression of her was quite different from that which he had expected, even before the jokesters had ribbed him in the saloon in Three Forks.

"Jonas said you told him you had business with me," she said."

"It can wait until after supper, if you like."

"No," she said. She looked directly at him, and pretty as she was, all blue eyes, fine blonde hair and smooth skin, soft, full mouth, he had the uncanny feeling she was indeed the expert markswoman she was said to be.

How does one tell a lovely young woman that one was an unwilling witness to the lynching of her brother?

"Well, Mr. Murdock?"

"I think you know why I am here," he said quietly. "I think you know who I am, and that I witnessed the death of your brother Jesse. The story about that terrible day must have spread clear through this country not long after it happened."

"It came to me by newspaper," she said. "It was the first knowledge I had of his death. In later editions of the paper I learned of a man named Murdock who left Ute Crossing shortly after the lynchings. It was said that he knew a great deal more about those lynchings than he had let on."

It was suddenly too quiet in that big room. Jim had the uneasy knowledge too that Jonas was not rattling around in the kitchen, and that he was not far behind Jim, maybe with a scatter-gun in his hands, or a cocked six-gun. He dropped his left hand into his coat pocket.

"Don't move, mister," said a dry voice a few feet behind him.

"I wasn't reaching for a hideout gun," said Jim. "Can I draw out my hand?"

Jessica nodded to Jonas.

Jim breathed easier as he withdrew his hand. He held out the Ridgewood tobacco sack with the stone in it. "This was about all I found of value in his clothing," he said.

She came to him and took the sack, her cool fingers touching his calloused hand. She opened the sack and emptied the stone into her left palm. For a moment she stared at the stone, and then she quickly turned away. Her shoulders shook a little.

"I'm sorry, ma'am," said Jim.

"You damned fool," hissed Jonas.

"It took you a long time," said Jessica at last.

Jim smiled. "It wasn't intentional," he said dryly.

She turned slowly. "You must be mad to come here."

Jim's eyes narrowed. "Why? Someone had to come and tell you. I am sorry you learned by other means. They told me about it in town."

"Who told you?"

"Man by the name of Kyle."

Her face tightened. "Chris Kyle," she said. She looked past Jim at Jonas. "Did Mr. Kyle, or any of the other *men* of Three Forks, tell you about me?"

Jim grinned. "They said you were right handy with a Winchester."

"You can copper that bet," said Jonas.

"I've had to build up that reputation," she said. "I'm not sorry for it."

"Can you have the little man take that gun out of my back?" said Jim. "What crime have I committed?"

She walked to the fireplace and held the stone up between her and the firelight, which caught and reflected the hidden glow of the semiprecious gem. "You were one of the men who murdered my brother," she said.

"That's a damned lie!" Jim said harshly.

"Take it easy!" snapped Jonas.

"Would I have come here into this damned trap if I had been one of those murderers?" said Jim. "What kind of fool do you take me for?"

"He might have a point there," said Jonas.

"You don't know everything I know, Jonas," said Jessica. "There was a man here last spring looking for you, Mr. Murdock. He came to this ranch. He was a deputy sheriff from Ute Crossing. He had a warrant for your arrest."

"On what charge?"

"Being part of that gang of lynchers. Stealing from the bodies of the dead."

"Well, I'll be double-damned," said Jim. "Begging your pardon, ma'am." He studied her. "Did he give his name?"

She nodded. "Meigs. Harlan Meigs."

"The man who was dead drunk the morning they took your brother and those other two men from the Ute Crossing jail."

"By God," said Jonas. "We never heard that one before!"

"Did he say that any of the others had been apprehended?" asked Jim.

"Most of them were unknowns."

"That's the biggest lie yet," said Jim angrily. "Every one of those men was well known in Ute Crossing!"

"None of their names were in the papers."

"No one would state that they had been in on it, that's why!" said Jim. "You don't know that town!"

"I know it well enough," she said bitterly.

"I'm beginning to see a little light coming through my thick skull. For some reason I'm not wanted back in Ute Crossing. It seems to me that someone tried to lay a trap for me here. A young woman whose brother was lynched, an expert riflewoman who supposedly had a habit of shooting first and asking questions afterward. Very neat. Perhaps if I hadn't managed to reach this place under cover of bad weather I'd have been shot when I put foot on your land."

"I wish I knew what you were talking about," said Jessica.

"Look," he said patiently. "Would it make sense for me to come here if I felt guilty for your brother's death? What logical reason would I have for coming here at all?"

"I have been wondering about that," she admitted. "A few months ago I might have shot you on sight. Now I don't know what to think."

"I have a suggestion," said Jim.

"Yes?"

"If you're as hungry as I am, I give my word I won't give you any trouble. There's a derringer in my right coat pocket, Jonas, but I won't reach for it. Take it out. Good! Now you can both sit at the other end of the table with six-guns beside your plates. The only weapons I want are a knife and a fork."

Jonas began to laugh. Even Jessica had a faint smile on her lovely face. "I guess we can afford to give a condemned man a good meal," she said.

"Ma'am," said Jim seriously, "I'm almost as good a talker as I am an eater. Let me tell you why I came here, and why it took me so long. About the time we ruin one of those pies out there you'll either believe me, or you can give me five minutes' start for the North Fork."

111

She nodded. Then she reached inside the bodice of her dress and withdrew a slender chain. She held it away from her breasts, and Jim saw a twin stone to the one he had brought from Ute Crossing, taken from the pocket of a dead boy to give to his twin sister. "We found these stones together when we were very young," she said softly. "Jesse always said they'd be good luck for us. He was wrong about that."

"Maybe he meant as long as you stayed together," said Jim.

She held the two stones side by side. "I never quite thought of it that way, Mr. Murdock," she said.

Chapter Thirteen

Jim Murdock led his horse up the narrow, twisting trail, following Jessica Lyle as she guided him up atop the great butte that seemed almost to hang over the North Fork far, far below, a glinting, sparkling stream that dashed across the stones in its shallow bed. The heavy rains of the past week had stopped at last, and the runoff was almost gone, although the ground was still soft with the soaking it had received. It was nice country, as Jonas had said. Plenty of water and grazing, but hardly any stock.

She rounded a turn in the trail and vanished. Jim slowly led the dun around the outthrust shoulder of the butte into a tangled jungle of scrub trees and brush that choked a great gash in the living rock, affording a shallow layer of earth for the tenacious roots of the growths. He climbed up a steep slope and then suddenly, as though someone had dropped the walls of the room, he found himself standing in the open, on naked, lichened rock, with a cool breeze sweeping about him, drying the sweat on his face. He looked about and whistled softly.

She turned and smiled. "It's worth the climb, isn't it, Jim?" she said. She pushed back her hat and let it drop to her back, hanging from the barbiquejo strap. The vagrant breeze toyed coyly with her fine hair. "You can smoke if you like."

He shoved back his own hat, watching her instead of the

magnificent western view that seemed to extend all the way into Utah. He rolled a cigarette and lighted it. She was right. The view alone was worth the whole ranch that lay below the butte, neatly encompassed by the North Fork, but the view wouldn't bring in the beans and bacon.

The sky was dotted with white cloud puffs that drifted, one after the other, like leaves on a stream, toward the west, while their fleeting shadows raced along the terrain below, up heights and down deep into the canyons, in a race that could never be lost or won. The air had a lift to it that hit a man's lungs and made him feel ten feet high.

He looked down at the ranch. A wraith of smoke drifted up from the big log house. The sun glinted from the windows. It was a good spread. There was timber to spare. A man could set up a sawmill and do some business. There was plenty of land for cattle. Water in plenty. Jim eyed the stream. Probably alive with trout. He smiled at the thought.

She sat down on a rock and wrapped her arms about her knees, tilting her head to one side to study him. "What's tickling you?" she asked.

"Nothing much. I was thinking there might be trout in that stream."

"There are. My father fished quite a bit. My mother sometimes said he fished too much, but then she never attempted to stop him. He was English and talked a lot at times about the fine fishing in Scotland."

"An educated man, no doubt."

"Yes. He had taught school in England, and later here in America. He was a college professor when he came west for his health, met my mother, and bought this place."

Jim blew a smoke ring. "A good rancher?"

She shrugged. "He got by. He liked his books. Mother was the real ramrod around here, but the two of them were happy." She smiled. "I'm more like her, I suppose."

"And Jesse?"

She looked away. "He was a great deal like Father. Sensitive, moody, more interested in books than in ranching. Father always said I should have been the male."

Jim shook his head. "What a terrible waste that would have been."

She flushed prettily. "I never wanted to be a man."

"Thank God for that," he said fervently.

"Mother didn't live long after Father passed on. As different as they were in many ways, they still seemed to have a great deal in common. Jesse had been planning to go to college, but when they were gone we found we had just

113

enough money to hold onto the place. This is a hard country. A woman can't very well run a ranch, although my mother seemed to do rather well at it, but then she had Father there to back her up. As refined and educated as he was, he was no coward. It didn't take the local men long to find that out. After the two of them passed away there was no choice for Jesse. He had to stay here and try to run the place." Her voice died away.

Jim remembered the bitter voice of Chris Kyle. *"There was only the two of them, and some of the bastards around here used to chase after Jessica, and the kid couldn't do anything about it. They drove that boy outa here."*

She looked out across the great span of country to the west. "Jesse said he had to leave. To find himself. I knew he never would. That is, he wouldn't find himself like the others. If Jesse had been raised in a city he would have risen to be a success. He couldn't adapt himself to this kind of life. Oh, I know what you're thinking! Why couldn't he adapt himself? You'd like this country and this ranch and everything about it if you had been raised here. Jesse was a loner. His only fault was that he was different. *So different. . . .*"

"And he never carried a gun?"

She shook her head. "I had to learn to shoot for the two of us. My father was an excellent shot, and my mother handled a gun as well as most ranch women. Jesse would have nothing to do with them." She looked at Jim. "He never shot anything in his life. The other boys used to haze him because he watched birds and animals rather than shoot them."

There was a long silence during which both of them were occupied with their own thoughts. Jim rolled another cigarette. "I'll be leaving in a day or two," he said quietly.

"To go back to Ute Crossing?"

"Yes."

"You can't bring Jesse back," she said.

"There's more to it than that, Jessica."

"The principle of the thing? You sound like my father now."

"Don't you agree with him?"

She looked away. "Someone is trying to kill you, Jim. Don't go back."

"I have to," he said. "I don't know whether Gil Drinkwater, Orlando Abeyta, and Jesse Lyle actually murdered Cass Crowley, and I know I can't bring the three of them back, but from what I have learned I find it difficult to believe

114

those three men did it. I nearly lost my own life on that same gallows hill because of circumstantial evidence, and I am beginning to believe that the circumstantial evidence against them was fixed. Jessica, those three men were lynched to cover up the real murderer or murderers. I mean to find out who actually did it, and to clear the names of Gil, Orlando, and Jesse."

"Does it really matter now?"

"It does to me." He smiled thinly. "I never got along too well with my own brother. I respected him, but I couldn't ever think like he could. I was the wild one."

She stood up. "So? A man who takes a full year out of his own life, rides hundreds of miles, and is trailed by men who would kill him if they could. A man who *had* to tell the kinfolk of those three lynched men their last words and actions. You are more like your brother than you'll admit."

She led the way down the steep, twisting trail, and there was no time to talk or look at the view. It took them the better part of an hour to reach the talus slope at the foot of the gaunt butte and then cross that into the cool shade of the trees. It was unseasonably warm weather, but the snow would be flying before too long, perhaps to block the passes to the east. Jim would have to leave before that time.

The North Fork rushed through the thick timber, drowning out all other sound. Jim led the horses to water. He turned to look at Jessica. The flat, whiplike crack of a rifle sounded above the rushing of the stream. Just as the rifle was fired Jim's dun tossed its head between Jim and the oncoming bullet. The dun died on its feet and fell heavily against Jim. He leaped clear of the horse and drove a shoulder against Jessica, felling her across a mossy log that lay on the damp ground. An instant later the rifle flatted off again, raising canyon echoes. The slug whipped within inches of Jim's head. He dived for cover as the slug slapped into a tree.

Then it was peaceful again. The stream rushed on. The clear waters were stained pink from the blood of the dun. Jessica's bay had taken off through the woods like the Devil beating tanbark. Jim studied the woods across the stream. Shafts of sunlight came slantingly through the timber and made spotlights on the ground. The rest of the woods were in shadow. There was neither sight nor sound of anyone. Whoever the ambusher was, he had either pulled leather out of there, or was waiting for another shot. Only by the grace of God had the dun raised his head to intercept that deadly slug.

Jessica lay flat, her soft cheek pressed against the grass. "Why?" she whispered.

"*Quién sabe?*" he said. His rifle was under the horse, pressed into the bottom of the shallow stream. It was too far for pistol range, and Jessica's bay had carried off her rifle.

Jim lay flat, peering across the stream from under the brim of his hat. He knew the slug had been meant for him. Jessica had been beyond a thick-boled tree. Besides, who would want to kill her? This was a question that was easier to answer in reference to Jim Murdock, but even so, it gave him an eerie feeling to know that they, whoever *they* were, had not given up on him. There was no one in Three Forks who would want to kill him. No, whoever it was had come from Ute Crossing. Who had notified them that Jim Murdock had returned from the dead to finish his self-imposed mission?

Jim bellied along the ground until he was in thick brush beyond a bend in the stream. He waded quickly across the stream and lay flat in brush on the far side. He drew his Colt and cocked it, inching his way across the ground until he could see the area where the ambusher should be if he had not left. There was no one in sight, no movement, no thickened shadow. Then he felt earth tremors beneath him, and he knew that a horse was being ridden swiftly away from the stream area. He stood up behind a tree and studied the area for five minutes until he was sure there was no one there.

Jim walked toward the place where the rifleman had waited. He looked across the stream and saw a thick tree trunk which had fallen long ago. Behind it he saw half a dozen cigarette butts, and twin depressions in the ground where boot toes had dug in. Jim knelt and then lay flat behind the log. Whoever had waited there must have known there was but one trail from the talus slope through the woods to the stream. He had known something else, that Jessica and Jim had been up on the butte. It had been a close thing; too damned close.

There was no other evidence except the crushed cigarette butts and the marks left by the ambusher. That and the dead dun staining the clear waters with his life's blood. It had been a good saddle horse, one of the best he had ridden since he had left Ute Crossing seemingly so long ago.

He waded across the stream and beckoned to Jessica. "Who knew we were going up on the butte?" he asked.

"Only Jonas."

116

He rubbed his scarred face. "Yeh," he said. He looked back across that peaceful-looking stream. "How well can you trust him?" he asked.

"It wasn't him," she said quickly.

"He might have told someone we were up there."

"No, Jim," she said firmly.

He looked at her and knew she was right.

"Now maybe you'll reconsider about going back to Ute Crossing," she said.

He did not answer. He caught Jessica's bay and then roped the dead dun, pulling it with the bay until he could get saddle and rifle from the dead animal. They rode double back to the ranch as the late afternoon sun slanted down into the huge canyon. The sun was gone when they reached the ranch, and a cold breeze drifted down the canyon.

"Goin' to be a hard winter," said Jonas from the porch. "Got lots of work to do before then. Sure could use a hand or two around here, Miss Jessica."

"No," she said.

"We can't keep on tryin' to keep this place up." Jonas glanced casually at Jim as Jim led the horse to the barn. "Where's the dun?"

Jessica told the little man. His face grew dark. "Dry-gulching! Bad enough they run off the stock and pester you without that going on."

"It wasn't meant for me," she said. "Whoever it was, he meant to kill Jim, Jonas."

"If he goes back to Ute Crossing he oughta have his head examined before it gets a bullet in it and spoils it."

"He's going," she said simply. "I can't stop him."

Jonas looked at the lovely young woman. "All the more reason he oughta have that head of his examined."

She flushed as she walked into the kitchen. "He must go," she said. She walked to the inner door and looked back. "Oh, Jonas! It isn't important anymore! Can't he understand that?"

Jonas shook his head. "You can't turn a man like him away from what he thinks he has to do."

"They'll kill him, Jonas!"

Jonas poked up the stove. He looked at her. "It takes a heap of killin' to get a man like Jim Murdock, and from the looks of him, he can do a mess of killin' himself if he has to."

The darkness had filled the canyon when Jim returned from the barn. He eyed the lighted windows. It reminded him of the time he had been fired upon when he had been sitting in Ben's little house outside of Ute Crossing. He

117

had never learned who had fired on him then either. He could hear Jonas singing "The Sago Lily" in the kitchen and got a scent of the evening meal. Something held him back. He stopped in the thick shadows beside an outbuilding, watching Jonas pass back and forth in front of the windows, a fair target for even a middling rifle shot.

He narrowed his eyes, probing into the darkness. The wind was seeping down the canyon, carrying man scent away from the dog Jonas kept chained at night in one of the outbuildings.

Something held him back from walking to the house. If he opened that kitchen door he'd be sharply silhouetted in light. There was the wariness of the wild animal in Jim Murdock. Ben had hit it on the head when he had said that Jim still had much of the lobo in him. Jim drifted through the darkness, a lean, scar-faced ghost of a man. He crouched and crossed to the front porch of the house. Jessica was in her room. There was no light in the living room. He crawled to the front door and softly opened it, wriggling inside. The door to the kitchen was closed, and no light showed except a thin crack at the bottom of the door. He walked softly to the door and tapped on it, stepping aside when Jonas opened it. "What the hell!" said the little man.

Jim drew him into the dark living room. "I smell something out there in the darkness," said Jim.

"Like what?"

"Like the son of a bitch who tried to kill me this afternoon."

"You see him? Hear him?"

"No."

"Then how the hell do you know he's there?"

Jim drew the little man close and looked into his wizened face, and the sight of that scarred mask Jim wore for a face shook Jonas more than he'd care to admit. "I *know!*" said Jim softly. He released the little man. "Tell Jessica to act like nothing is going on. You keep up your usual work. Is there a rifle in the house?"

"Mine. I'll get it. Best damned saddle gun I ever had."

Jim drifted out into the thick, pre-moon darkness, working his way into the timber a hundred yards in front of the brightly lighted house. He took to the ground and inched along until he was well into the timber. Now and then he would stop and raise his head, testing the windy darkness with his senses. The wind shifted and brought the bittersweet odor of woodsmoke to him, mingled with the good aroma of food.

Half an hour drifted past on the moaning wind.

Jim lay behind a rock outcropping. Maybe he was a fool. There was a sudden flare of light not thirty feet away from Jim. A hand cupped a match to a cigarette, softly illuminating a hard-looking face. Then the match went out, and all Jim could see was the alternate lighting and darkening of the face as the man drew in on the cigarette. Damned fool! He was so sure of himself. Jim recognized him from somewhere, but he wasn't sure where. Ute Crossing? No. Meadows? No. He lay flat and cudgeled his memory. Then it came to him. This was the drunk he had seen in the saloon the day he had arrived at Three Forks!

Jim rubbed his scarred face. The rifle was at his side, half-cocked, and he could drive a .44/40 slug into the man before he'd hear the shot. He heard the man move. The cigarette was ground out. Softly, ever so softly, like a hunting cat, the man moved through the motte toward the house, until he was fifty yards from it. He held a rifle in his hands. He was so interested in the house that he never saw the man standing behind the tree fifty feet behind him, watching his every move, nor did he realize his shoulders and head were etched against the darkness by the light from the windows.

Jim looked beyond the man. Jonas was still moving back and forth. He saw Jessica come into the room. She was still wearing her hat. It was difficult to see that she was a woman from that distance. Suddenly the dog barked. The man raised his rifle, moved it a little, and tilted his head to get a sight.

"Drop that rifle!" snapped Jim.

The man swung and the rifle spat flame and smoke toward Jim. The bullet almost touched Jim's right cheek. He fired from the hip. The big slug smashed into the man's chest. He grunted, spun about, dropped the rifle, and fell heavily. The twin rifle reports slammed back and forth in the canyon and then fled muttering to die away. The wind whipped a tendril of acrid-smelling smoke across Jim's face.

The lights blinked out in the house. The dog went wild. Jim walked forward, then knelt beside the man. He snapped a match on his thumbnail and held it over the man's face. A pair of staring, sightless eyes looked up into his. Jim fanned out the match. A door slammed up at the house. Someone ran across the porch and toward Jim.

"Jim! Jim!" cried Jessica. *"Jim!"*

"It's all right," he called out.

119

She was in his arms with such a force that she staggered him. He dropped the rifle and held her close.

Jonas trotted through the darkness with a six-gun in his hand. "You all right, Jim?" he called.

"Yes, Jonas."

Jonas knelt beside the dead man and lighted a match. He whistled softly. "Monk!" he said.

"You know him?" asked Jim.

Jonas shrugged. "I've seen him around. He's a drifter. No one knows where he came from. He always seemed to have a dollar in his pocket. He'd come and go for long periods of time. Why would he want to kill you?"

Jim looked down at the dead man. "Someone hired him to do it. The only time I ever saw him was in the saloon in Three Forks. The one where Les is the barkeeper."

Jonas stood up. "He got his orders from somewhere. Ute Crossing, likely."

"But from who?"

"There's the question," said Jonas.

Jim nodded. "He didn't have time to go back there. Maybe someone came here to tell him what to do."

Jonas looked at Jim. "There's a company telegraph line between here and Ute Crossing."

"That might be the answer."

Jonas nodded. "Ben Cole is the operator. He'd have a record of any messages sent."

"Can we get a look at those records?"

Jonas grinned. "I can. Ben and I served together in the war. First Colorado Volunteers. Ben would do anything for me." Jonas looked down at Monk. "What about him?"

An idea had drifted into Jim's mind. Monk was about his size, build, and coloring. "A dead man can move around for a time without being expected," he said.

Jonas stared at him. "You gone loco?"

"Not yet. I have hopes. You go into Three Forks in the morning and find out what, if any, message Monk sent out. Keep your mouth shut about this. Find out where Monk is supposed to be. When you get back I'll tell you what I plan to do."

They carried Monk to an outbuilding and covered his stiffening body. Jessica was waiting for them in the house. "Jim," she said pleadingly. "Must you go back to Ute Crossing?"

"Yes."

"I won't let you go."

The look in his eyes silenced her even before his words. "I'm going, Jessica," he said flatly.

"We never did get to eat," said Jonas.

"After a killing?" said Jessica.

"Far's I'm concerned, Miss Jessica," said Jonas, "it's like a celebration when you kill a dry-gulcher."

"Amen," said Jim.

Chapter Fourteen

Jonas was back by noon of the next day with a wagon-load of supplies and a nose full of news. Jim helped him unload the wagon. "Monk sent a telegram the day you got to Three Forks," said the little man. "Got there just when Ben was closing the office. Message was sent to Ute Crossing. *'Consignment arrived,'* it read, *'please advise disposition.'* The next day there was a reply from Ute Crossing. *'Dispose of merchandise as previously directed,'* it read."

Jim slid a box of canned goods onto a storeroom shelf and wiped the sweat from his face. "Who had signed it?" he asked.

"It was from a Ute Valley Mercantile Company. Signed by a man named Alfred Hitchins."

Jim turned slowly, and his eyes were like twin lances boring into Jonas' eyes. "Alfred Hitchins?" he said softly.

"That was the name. You know him?"

Jim nodded. "I know him," he said. He seemed to see the round, smooth face of the man in the reflection of a can of peaches. Peaches thick in syrup. Alfred Hitchins, for all his good works, had always been a little too syrupy to suit Jim. The Reverend Matthew Jarvis was next to God in Ute Crossing, and Alfred Hitchins was next to the reverend.

"What do you aim to do?"

Jim lifted a sack of flour and placed it on a shelf. "Saddle a horse, Jonas," he said over his shoulder.

"For you?"

"For you, amigo. Go back to town. Send this wire to

121

Alfred Hitchins, Ute Valley Mercantile Company: '*Merchandise disposed of as ordered.*' Sign it '*Monk.*' "

They finished unloading the supplies, rolled cigarettes, and lighted them. Jonas eyed Jim. "You're taking a hell of a risk," he said.

"No worse than if I had gone back there without doing it."

Jonas grinned. "It's a prime idea," he said. "If you're right in your hunch they'll think you're dead."

Jim nodded. "That's why I wanted to save Monk. What did you find out about him?"

"Les told me he had left for Utah some days ago, and said he wouldn't likely be back until spring, if he came back at all."

"*Bueno!* We'll dress him in some of my old clothes and plant him."

"You mean bury him?"

Jim shook his head. "Put him where he'll be sure to be found. On the other side of town."

"Hell! That ain't so bright! They can see he ain't you."

Jim blew a smoke ring. "Dead body lying out in the woods gets the face eaten away first, doesn't it?"

"We can't take a chance they will eat it."

Jim looked at him. "A man could fake it, couldn't he?"

Jonas swallowed. "Yeh. A dirty job, Jim."

Jim spat. "It would have been a helluva lot dirtier job if he had killed me that day at the river, or if he had killed Jessica by mistake last night."

"I get your point. Leave it to me. There's only one thing, Jim. People in town know you came out here."

"They don't know I stayed here."

"Still looks bad for us."

Jim shrugged. "Shoot one round out of a pistol. Here, take mine and I'll take Monk's. It's a good one. Better than mine. Put the pistol in his hand, or near it."

"Suicide, eh?"

"You're getting brighter every minute, Jonas."

"What happens when you come back? If you do come back?"

"They made a mistake in identifying the body, is all."

Jonas flipped away his cigarette. "It might work at that, Jim."

Jim grinned like a lobo. "It will work long enough for me to do my job in Ute Crossing." He rubbed his scarred face. "By God," he added. "Alfred Hitchins! Who would have believed it?"

He said good-bye to Jessica at dusk that same day. Jonas had told him of a trail over the butte that would take him to the foot of the pass which he could cross that night. There would be a moon. The weather was making up, hinting at more rain. He could be across the pass by dawn with a bit of luck, hole up on the other side during daylight hours, then move on during the night. In three to four days he could be in Ute Crossing.

He kissed Jessica and drew her close.

"You'll come back?" she asked.

"Yes."

She looked up at him. "Maybe you'll want to stay in Ute Crossing," she said quietly.

Jim shook his head. "Never. There's nothing there for me now. My brother is gone. When my job is done I'll be back."

He kissed her again and swung up on the chunky roan Jonas had selected for him. "Adios," he said. He touched the horse with his spurs and rode off into the windy darkness.

"*Vaya con Dios,*" she said.

The wind shifted, moaning down the valley, and bringing with it a hint of the cold rain to follow before the dawn.

"He'll be back," said Jonas.

She did not answer. She walked to the house and entered it. Jonas rolled a cigarette. He lighted it. "He has to come back, God," he said softly. "For her. . . ."

The rain had started the dawn of the day Jim reached the eastern entrance of the pass. Warrior Peak, towering high to his left, had a skullcap of snow on it. In a matter of weeks, perhaps, the first snows of the season would fall. He rode through the dark, wet nights, holing up in the daytime under the tarp Jonas had given him, drinking coffee and smoking, trying to fit together the pieces of the puzzle he had blundered into by becoming an unwilling witness to a triple lynching. The enigma was Alfred Hitchins. "Deacon" Hitchins . . . the man who had helped Ben Murdock get his education after he had been crippled in his fight to clear Jim of murder charges. The man who had fought against public opinion to get Ben his job as schoolteacher in Ute Crossing, and who had won his fight. A man respected by one and all for his business ability, his civic pride, and his support of the local church. A man said to be as close to God as a man could be within reason. "Jesus wept," he had said when he had seen the lynchers take those three men up the gallows hill.

The rain was a fine, misty drizzle when Jim Murdock passed his brother's house on the banks of roaring Warrior Creek. The place was nothing but a blackened shell dimly seen through the mist. Warrior Creek swirled blackly beneath the creaking bridge. It was here that Ben had gone to his death over the low rail into the dark, cold waters, not to be found until the spring, on land that had once belonged to the Murdocks.

There was only one man he could go to in Ute Crossing and be sure of secrecy. Meany Gillis. It was well after midnight when he entered the town. Here and there along the main street he could see watery-looking yellow light as a saloon or two remained in business. One of them was the Grape Arbor.

There was a light in one of the rear windows of the Ute Valley Mercantile Company. Jim looked at it thoughtfully as he kneed the tired roan into an alleyway and then led him toward the rear of Slade's Livery Stable, where Meanwell Gillis held sway. Meany lived in a set of rooms built into the livery stable, a little strong-smelling, but comfortable and cozy, and besides, as Meany had always said, he preferred the company of horses and dogs to that of many people.

The alleyway was empty and dark. Jim walked around the side of the big frame building and tapped on the window of Meany's bedroom. The window was up a few inches. "Meany!" called Jim.

Bedsprings squeaked. "Who's that?" said Meany in a frightened voice.

"Jim. Jim Murdock."

"Oh, my God! You've come back from the dead! You always was a restless sort. I didn't think you was that restless."

Jim grinned. "Meany," he said softly. "It was a dodge. A trick to throw them off the trail."

Feet padded on the floor, and Meany's familiar, homely face appeared, white as a sheet. "Lemme touch you, Jim," he said. "Just to make sure." A thin hand felt Jim's arm. "Keno!"

"Open up the back door and let me get my horse inside."

Meany opened the back door. He peered up and down the alleyway. "Anyone see you?"

"No."

The door swung shut and was barred. "You hungry, Jim?"

"No. But cold as ice."

"I got something to take care of that. Take care of your hoss."

Jim came into Meany's little combination kitchen and sitting room after he had unsaddled and rubbed down the roan. The liveryman had drawn the curtains and pulled down the shade. He handed Jim a tumbler full of spirits. "You got guts comin' back here," he said.

Jim sipped the whiskey. "How'd you find out I was dead?"

"The story was all over town a few days ago. I don't know where it started. That's the second time it came around."

"When was the first time?"

Meany shrugged. "Damned near a year ago. They said you was killed down in Mexico somewheres."

Jim touched the scar on his right cheek. "I damned near was. Anyone miss Lyss, Slim, and Jules around here?"

Meany stared at Jim. His jaw dropped. "You!" he said.

Jim smiled thinly. "It was them or me, Meany."

"Wasn't nothing said about them. They was just supposed to have left. Rumor come that Lyss was murdered by bandits in Las Cruces, and Slim and Jules disappeared in Chihuahua or somewheres. They meant to kill you then?"

Jim nodded. "Why did they come after me? Who sent them, Meany?"

Meany poured a drink. He was pale again. "Jesus God," he mumbled. "Three hardcases if there ever was any. You took care of all *three* of them?"

"Two of them. I had a little help with the third."

Meany sat down heavily. He drained his glass. "Thank God you was always a friend of mine, James."

Jim leaned forward. "A man was ordered to kill me at Three Forks a few days ago, Meany. The order came from Ute Crossing."

Meany wiped his mouth. "Who sent it?"

"I think it was sent by Alfred Hitchins."

Meany was less surprised than Jim thought he should be. "I never liked that sanctimonious son of a bitch," he said. "Never could stand a man who's always telling you how honest he is. You sure about that?"

Jim told him of the cryptic telegraph messages.

"Sounds logical," said Meany.

"But why?" said Jim.

Meany swirled the liquor in his glass. "Beats the hell out of me," he said. "There is one thing I do know. 'Bout a year or so ago before you came back, he was having financial trouble. Rumor had it he was in hock for quite a bit. Someone had a big note on him and was hounding him for the money."

"Like who?" said Jim.

Meany looked into his glass. "Cass Crowley," he said. He

125

looked up at Jim. "After them three drifters killed Cass, Hitchins seemed to be doing all right again."

"The note would have been found in Crowley's papers," said Jim. "Hitchins would have been forced to pay the estate."

"If they found the note," said Meany. "Far's I know, it never was found. Hitchins denied there ever had been a loan."

"Seems to me it would have been a big break for him if Cass Crowley had died."

Meany looked up again. "*Murdered,*" he said.

"By three drifters. One of them a drunk who wouldn't carry a six-gun and was supposedly unarmed when he came to the valley of the Ute. A Mexican who had wanted to be a priest and was afraid of firearms. A frightened, sensitive kid who likely fell in with the other two because they thought the same way he did."

"What are you driving at? You mean them three who was hung?"

Jim nodded. "It has taken me a year to find out about them, Meany. If those three men killed Crowley, it was certainly out of character."

"Then who done it if they didn't?"

Jim stood up and drained his glass. "That's exactly why I came back to Ute Crossing," he said.

Meany shivered. "I don't envy you."

Jim picked up his hat. "Keep your mouth shut about me," he said. "Can you put me up here at night?"

"Sure thing! Where you goin' now?"

Jim smiled. "Looks like Al Hitchins is working late."

Meany spat into the garboon. "He always is. Got a Bible in one hand and his cashbox in the other."

"Is Van Lassen still around town?"

Meany nodded. "Don't ever seem to work, but always has dinero. Beats me how he does it."

Jim flipped his cigarette butt into the garboon. "I wonder," he said quietly. He left the room, followed by Meany. He passed a dusty buggy and stopped suddenly to look at it.

"Yes," said Meany from behind Jim. "It's Ben's." He placed a hand on the dashboard. "I had it hauled here. Kept it for you, Jim, in case you wanted it."

Jim looked back at him. "Thanks. You keep it, Meany. I have no use for it."

"When you get back, providing someone don't put a slug into you, I'll tell you something about that buggy."

Jim nodded. He let himself out into the drizzle and heard

Meany close the door behind him and drop the bar. He padded through the pasty mud, cutting swiftly across the cross streets. Ute Crossing was quiet beneath the cold drizzle. The faint thudding of a mechanical piano came from the Grape Arbor as Jim passed behind it. He reached the rear of the Ute Valley Mercantile Company. The light was still on in the rear office. Jim peered into the rain-streaked window. A man was seated at a rolltop desk, hard at work on some papers. There was no mistaking the plump back of the merchant and the bald spot at the back of his head.

Jim gently tried the back door, but it was locked. He walked along the other side of the building until he found a warped window. He forced a piece of wood under the sash and pried upward. The lock snapped. He eased up the window and stepped inside. He could see a faint streak of light from the rear of the long building. Cautiously he worked his way past piles of sacks and ranks of boxed goods until he found himself in the aisle that led to the offices in the rear of the establishment. He paused, listening to the rain drumming on the tin roof. There was neither sound nor sign of anyone else in the place besides Hitchins.

Jim walked softly to the rear hall that opened to offices on either side. Hitchins did a big business. It was the same type of business Jim's father had successfully run until Jim's trouble with the law. An odd thought came to Jim. Al Hitchins had been small potatoes in this line of work until Jim's father's business had failed because of people talking. It was only after his father had failed that Hitchins had gained prominence in the business. He had taken over the lucrative Crowley account, one of the mainstays of the Murdock business. Maybe it had been Hitchins himself who had started the talk against Jim's father. People listened to Alfred Hitchins.

Jim walked softly into the hallway and stood in the open door of Hitchins' private office. The merchant's pen scratched on. Jim studied him. It wasn't going to be easy to beard Al Hitchins in his own den. It seemed ridiculous to suspect this godly man of having anything to do with ordering a killer to get rid of a man who stood in the way. It was loco, and yet. . .

Hitchins stopped writing. He raised his head. He sat still for a moment or two, then shook his head and started writing again. Jim stood there, boring a hole in the bald spot at the back of Hitchins' head with his cold eyes. Hitchins stopped writing again. He sat there for another moment, and then he slowly turned his head, to see an apparition standing in the doorway. A tall, gaunt man, scarred on both lean cheeks, with granite-hard eyes looking at him with an unblinking stare. Hitchins sharply drew in his breath. His face went fish belly white. Slowly he extended a hand toward Jim and shook his eyes. "For the love of God," he husked. "Go away! I didn't want to do it! Go away! I'll forswear my God if you'll go away!"

Jim did not move. He tried not to blink.

Hitchins began to tremble. His mouth opened and closed. "They made me do it! They told me I was in it as deep as they were! I had to do it! Don't you understand! All I wanted was that note from Cass Crowley. That was all! I didn't want to put a bullet into his head!" He stood up and held out both hands, as though to ward off the cold, basilisk stare of the man he was sure had come back from the dead. Then he shook spasmodically. He fell to his knees. His head jerked and he cried out in savage pain, gripping his left side. He fell heavily and stared at Jim with unblinking eyes. Spittle drooled from his slack mouth.

Jim walked toward him. "Who made you do it?" he asked.

The man tried to speak. His breathing was sharp and erratic.

"Talk, damn you!" said Jim.

"They said I *had* to put a bullet into his head! All three of us did it! It was a pact with the Devil!"

"Who were the other two?" demanded Jim.

Hitchins' eyes widened. "You're alive," he whispered.

Jim nodded. "Tell me," he said.

Hitchins raised his head and suddenly it fell again. He stiffened, then relaxed, and his eyes still looked at Jim, but they did not see him. They would never see anything on earth again.

Jim stood up. "Score one," he said quietly. All he knew now was that the three men who had been lynched had not killed Cass Crowley, but who had been the other two men who had put bullets into the rancher's head? He rubbed his newest scar and looked down at Hitchins. God had dealt out his own kind of justice to this man. It was just as well. Jim wanted no more blood on his own hands. Justice, yes, but not blood. . . . . No one would know Jim had been there. They would find Hitchins in the morning, dead of a heart attack. The whole town would mourn. Likely his two partners in murder would breathe more freely. Hitchins had probably been the weak link in the chain. They would breathe more freely, but they did not know that retribution was stalking the wet streets of Ute Crossing in the guise of a man who was thought to be dead of a dry-gulcher's bullet.

Jim left the same way he had come, lowering the window against the rain. He padded into the alleyway. His work was done for this night, at least. He heard the thudding of the mechanical piano in the Grape Arbor as he neared it, and then the sound stopped. Jim stopped beside a rear window. A man was walking toward the mechanical piano, flipping a coin into the air and catching it again. Beyond him were the hunched backs of other men at the long bar. The man reached out with the coin to insert it in the piano slot. He stared at the rain-streaked window and saw a lean, scarred face staring at him, and then it was gone. Barney Kessler's eyes widened. The coin fell to the floor from nerveless fingers and rolled under the piano. Barney turned on his heel and ran to the bar and filled a glass, which he downed in one gulp.

Van Lassen looked at Barney. "What the hell is the matter with you?" he said sarcastically. "You see a ghost?"

Barney slowly wiped his mouth. His eyes were glassy with tanglefoot and fear. "I don't know," he said slowly. "*I don't know....*"

Baldy Victor grinned. "Oughta cut you off, Barney," he said.

Buck Grant spat into the filthy garboon. "Who was it you seen, Barney?" he asked.

Barney refilled the glass. "I'll swear to Christ it was Jim Murdock! Them eyes! The scars!"

Van grinned. "Jim Murdock had only one scar," he said. He drew a thick finger down the left side of his face. "There!"

Buck laughed. "Maybe Monk give him another one," he said. "Afore he died, that is."

Baldy studied Barney. "Maybe he did see something," he said curiously. He walked around the end of the bar and peered through the window. He unbarred and opened the back door and peered up and down the muddy alleyway, with the rain sleeting down, cold and penetrating. He grinned, and then the grin faded. He felt something in the atmosphere, something that sent a crawling chill through him. He closed and barred the door, picked up Barney's coin, and dropped it into the piano slot. The piano began to thud out a tune. Baldy walked back to the bar.

"Well?" said Lassen.

"Nothing," said Baldy. But for the rest of the night he kept shifting his eyes toward that back door when he was sure no one was watching him.

Chapter Fifteen

Jim Murdock knelt in the damp straw that covered the livery stable floor, holding a lantern while Meany Gillis, underneath Ben Murdock's buggy, pointed out something to Jim. "The team was found at the edge of town still pulling the front wheels, Jim," said Meany. "The rest of the buggy was found in the creek. The rail had been busted as it went through. I pulled out the buggy body and rear wheels and had it hauled here. I already had the team and the front wheels. I had a little free time one day, so I started work on it. I noticed marks on the wood around where the kingbolt goes through. Like someone had been sawing or filing. Then I finds the upper part of the kingbolt still in its socket. It was a good sound bolt, Jim, but it was in two pieces, and all I had was the upper piece."

"It broke, and caused the accident?"

Meany shook his head. He reached up inside the buggy and handed Jim the upper part of a kingbolt. "Take a good look at it," he said.

Jim held it close to the lantern. A cold feeling came over him as he saw file marks on the bolt.

Meany crawled out. "I went back to the bridge and found this." He handed Jim the rest of the bolt. Jim studied it. It had file marks on it, and at one edge was a slightly raised lip of metal as though the bolt had been filed almost through, leaving just enough so that the strain on it would eventually snap it off.

Meany wiped his hands. "You know how fast Ben drove. Likely he come out of his gate and turned hard, hit the bridge at a good clip, and the bolt busted right there. Talk about timing!"

Jim looked up. "But why, Meany?"

Meany held out his hands, palms upward. "After you left Ben did a lot of talking about those three men that got lynched. He was talking about justice before they got lynched. Looks like you put a head on his suspicions, or whatever they were. Ben might have been on to something at that.

130

Anyways, he was drowned before he could do anything about it. A week or so later his house goes up in flames. People said drifters had been bunking there and accidentally set it afire."

"Maybe there was something in there that might have pinned the guilt on whoever killed Cass Crowley."

"Mebbe," said the liveryman. "Whatever *might* have been there is gone now. No one will ever know now."

Jim rolled a cigarette and lighted it. He fanned out the match. "You're wrong there," he said. "I told you Hitchins was in on it. He implied there were two others. They're likely still around here, Meany. I won't stop until I find out who they were. This is a personal thing now. They murdered Cass Crowley and they murdered my brother. That type never stops killing to cover up, and the first killing is the hardest. After that they get easier and easier."

"Hard to figure out why they killed Cass," said Meany.

"We know why Hitchins was in on it. Money was his real god. Cass could have ruined Hitchins. Maybe money had something to do with the others as well."

Meany led the way to his rooms and poured two glasses of whiskey. "Maybe not," he said quietly. "Cass was in a lot of things. Finance, politics, and anything else he had a mind to get into. Cass liked power of any kind. You know damned well there never was an appointment in this county he wasn't behind, one way or another."

"You can say that about the whole state," said Jim dryly.

Meany sipped his drink. "If Cass stood in Al Hitchins' way, maybe the other two hombres what killed him felt the same way he did. Cass was as tough as whang leather when you crossed him. Many a coming man run into old Cass when he wasn't feelin' too well, said the wrong thing, and ruined his whole career. Just like that!"

"Just like that," repeated Jim. "Like who?" he added.

Meany laughed. "Well, they can be numbered by the dozens. I run into trouble with him once and was lucky enough to get off the hook." He grinned. "One time I took a repaired surrey out to Brady Short's place. I went up to the house to get paid and heard Brady sounding off to his wife. He was cutting ol' Cass to ribbons, being as how ol' Cass wasn't there. Seems like Brady had been counting on Cass to back him up politically. Brady could hardly get anywheres without Cass backing his play. You know the old story. The 'boy wonder' of the Ute Valley. Marries old Whitcomb's daughter, getting a nice piece of change in the process, plus

131

that cliff dwelling of a house. By God, he's ambitious, and his wife is worse, or so they say."

"Take it easy, Meany," said Jim quietly. He swirled the liquor in his glass and then looked up at the liveryman. "When did all this take place, Meany?"

Meany looked at the ceiling and closed one eye. "About a year and a half ago. No! It was less than that. It was late summer of last year."

"Just before those three men were arrested for the killing of Cass Crowley."

"Yeh." Meany stared at Jim. "You mean?"

Jim finished his drink. "I don't know," he said. "Who would have suspected Alfred Hitchins?"

"Who indeed?" echoed Meany.

Something came back to Jim. The night he had gone out to Brady Short's house at the lawyer's request, only to find that the man was gone, Ann was in her cups and willing to play games with Jim. She had practically thrown herself at him. An icy, evil feeling crept through him. She was ambitious. Meany himself had just said that. She'd get behind a man and drive him on. Supposing she had been grooming Brady for big things and the fool had antagonized the one man in the county he had to have behind him to win political success. She had warned Jim to leave the country. Brady Short had never intended to be at the house when Jim arrived, or perhaps he had been in the house, keeping out of the way while he let his lovely wife bargain with Jim, using her lush body as bait. If a man was making love to Ann Short he'd damned well forget anything else he had in mind at the time.

Meany filled the glasses. He looked at Jim. "You're sure talkative tonight, James."

Jim took the refilled glass. The whiskey had no effect on him. Ann's last cast of the dice had been the blunt invitation to Jim to visit her in Denver. "Did Mrs. Short go to Denver last fall, Meany?" he asked. Meany would know. Nothing much went on in the valley of the Ute without Meany knowing about it.

Meany laughed. "Hell, no! She's hardly been outa that house. They say she's always on a high lonesome up there while Brady's chasin' around doing his political maneuvers. Sits up most of the night, they say, dozing in a chair, with a wine decanter next to her. When it's empty she gets another, and another. . . ."

"Every night?" asked Jim.

"Just about."

Jim emptied his glass. "Let me have a horse," he said.

132

"This late?"

Jim stood up. "I haven't much time," he said.

"You've done enough tonight."

Jim shook his head. "If I'm not back by daylight I'll hide out in the hills. I don't want to be seen. Not yet. . . ."

The streets of Ute Crossing were empty as Jim Murdock rode north out of town, heading into the slanting rain. The last time he had passed that way the road had been iron hard in the grip of the winter's first freeze. That time was close again.

This time he did not see lights in the huge house until he was close to it. The shades had been drawn in the sitting room that opened off the huge parlor where he had last talked to Ann Short, but he saw thin lines of light about the edges of the shades. There were no other lights on in the house. He tethered the horse to the picket fence and softly opened the gate. He walked to the front steps and softly padded to the side window of the sitting room. Through the narrow slit at the side of the shade he could see into the room. A woman sat in an armchair, facing a dying fire in the grate. A decanter stood on the little table beside her, and even as he looked he saw her fill a glass with wine.

He walked to the parlor windows. One of them was open a few inches. He eased it up and stepped inside, careless of the mud that stained the thick carpeting. He walked into the wide hallway and looked up the stairway. The house was dark and quiet. Jim crossed the parlor and softly slid back the sliding door that separated parlor from sitting room. The woman did not move.

Jim walked forward a little. "Ann," he said softly.

For a moment she did not move, and then slowly she turned to look at him. Shock fled across her flushed face, and then she smiled, although there was no mirth in her great eyes. "I knew they'd never kill you," she said.

"You're not surprised to see me, then?"

She shrugged. "Why should I be?" She glanced at the wine decanter. "I don't get surprised at anything anymore, Jim."

She had changed, even in the space of one year. Her face was flushed looking, and not from the bloom of health. Her once clear eyes had a slightly glassy look to them, and her hands trembled a little until she clasped them firmly in her lap.

"Where's Brady?" he said.

She laughed. "Out on his political maneuvers. Likely in one of the back rooms of the Ute House with one of the high-class doxys who ply their business there."

133

"Not Brady," he said dryly.

She sipped her wine. "Brady likes his women from the gutter," she said. "They give him what he wants. I won't."

She was almost stinking drunk. She wouldn't care what she said. "Did you ever go to Denver?" he asked.

She shook her lovely head. "I had no reason to go after you left," she said.

"You really wanted me to meet you there?"

A log snapped in the fireplace, and a little cloud of ashes drifted out onto the carpet. She laughed softly. "No," she said. "Does that sting your ego, Jim? Your man's ego?"

"Not really," he said. "Whose idea was it?"

She emptied her glass and refilled it. "I think you already know," she said.

"I want to be sure."

She nodded. "It was him. He was scared to death of you. I told him to kill you or have you killed. He's yellow."

"You would have done what you told him to do if you were in his position?"

She looked at him with thoughtful eyes. "Why not?" she said coldly. "He should have known he'd never sidetrack you. If you had that man's legal mind and his appearance, with your guts and me to back you up you'd have been governor someday. He lost his nerve. He could have gone a long way. I agreed to ask you to meet me in Denver just to help him." She wrinkled her nose and shook her head. "Making a whore out of myself to help him. Putting myself at your feet after you walked out on me." She hiccupped.

"That's a switch," he murmured. "You never intended to marry me, Ann. You had bigger game in mind."

"Go to hell," she said.

"Was Brady mixed up in the killing of Cass Crowley?"

"Ask him," she said shortly. "He's standing right behind you."

Jim turned slowly. Brady Short stood in the doorway wearing a wet slicker, his hat dark with rainwater. His face was pasty white beneath its tan. A nickel-plated, short-barreled Colt was in his right hand, pointing at Jim's guts. His handsome face was set, and there was haunting fear in his dark eyes. "What are you doing here?" he said in a low voice.

"Just a social call, Brady."

"At two o'clock in the morning?"

Jim smiled. "My, my! Is it that late?"

"Why didn't you stay away?" asked the lawyer. "Why did you have to come back, grinning like a death's-head at the feast?"

"You did your best to keep me away," said Jim. He glanced at Ann. "In more ways than one. The game is up, Brady."

"What do you know? What can you prove?"

Jim smiled. "Al Hitchins told me the whole story," he said. The shot struck home. Brady stared at Jim. "He doesn't know anything," he said.

"He said you forced him into the deal. That he was in it as deep as you were. That Cass Crowley had turned against you, and that you knew damned well you'd never get anywhere in this state politically without Cass backing up your play. You had to kill him, Brady, or your career was shot, just as Al Hitchins had to be in on the deal to keep from being ruined financially."

"For God's sake!" said Brady. "You devil! No one outside of the three of us knew that!"

Ann stood up and began to fill her glass. "You'd better kill him, Brady," she said. "It's your only chance."

The lawyer's finger tightened on the trigger. Jim wet his dry lips. Did he have a chance to draw and shoot before Brady got up his nerve?

"Go on, Brady," taunted Ann. "Show us you're a man! He's all that stands in your way. You helped kill Cass Crowley. The first one is the easiest one. Go on!"

"Shut your drunken mouth," said her husband.

She laughed. "One little press of that trigger and you're on your way again. Who can prove otherwise? You're a lawyer. You know I can't testify against you. I'll even help you, Brady. I'll say he came in here drunk and tried to rape me. This is your last chance, you fool!"

He drew in a deep breath and raised the pistol. For a moment he looked into Jim's eyes, and then his gaze wavered. He raised the pistol again. The empty wine decanter was hurled past Jim, and it struck Brady's gun arm. The pistol exploded, driving a slug into the floor at Jim's feet. He ran forward through the swirling smoke to grapple with Brady. Brady swung the smoking pistol up and down, cutting viciously at Jim's head. Jim deflected the blow with his forearm, but the gun still struck his face, staggering him. Brady whirled and ran. The front door was opened and then slammed. Feet thudded on the gravel walk, and a moment later the thudding of hoofs came back to the two people in the sitting room.

Jim wiped the blood from his face. He turned to look at her. "Why?" he said.

She shrugged. "I couldn't live with him any longer, Jim," she said. "I wanted to see if he had the guts to kill you."

"Thanks," he said dryly.

"How far can he get?"

Jim held out his hands, palms upward. "Brady Short is too well known to get very far. He'll run and keep on running, but someday they'll find him. He'll live a hell on earth until they do find him. Who is the third man, Ann?"

She walked to a side table and picked up a full wine decanter. "I saved your life tonight," she said over her shoulder. "Isn't that enough?"

"No."

She turned. "If I told you I didn't know would you believe me?"

He studied her. "Yes."

"You're walking a thin line, Jim. There are men in Ute Crossing who have sworn to kill you. You were nearly killed tonight. Get out of town and keep going, Jim."

"I can't do that."

She filled her wineglass and studied the ruby contents. "I didn't think you would. Good luck, Jim."

"I'm sorry about Brady," he said.

"I'm not."

He turned on a heel and walked from that house and he knew he'd never enter it again or see her again. He closed the front door and walked to his horse through the cold, drifting rain. He mounted and rode south toward Ute Crossing. "Score two," he said to the night.

She had parted the curtains to see him ride off. *"If you had had that man's legal mind and his appearance, with your guts and me to back you up you'd have been governor someday."* She drew the curtains and walked back to her chair, moved the wine decanter a little closer, and stared unseeingly into the dying fire.

Chapter Sixteen

The wind shifted just before dawn and carried the rain off with it. With the coming of daylight the wind died away altogether, and left a drifting mist in the bottoms of the Ute that seeped through the streets of Ute Crossing.

Jim awoke to Meany's shaking hand and low voice. "Rise

and shine," said the liveryman. "It's nigh nine o'clock. Murray Cullin just came into town and is at the jail."

Jim rolled over on the cot and looked up at Meany. "How's the weather?"

Meany rubbed a hand over the fogged panes of window glass. "Never seen the like of it in many a year. You can hardly see acrost the street."

"Suits me," said Jim. He sat up and accepted a cup of Arbuckle's from Meany.

"This fog won't stop a bullet, James."

"They have to see me to shoot at me."

"You sure no one else outside of Al Hitchins, Brady and Ann Short has seen you?"

Jim grinned. "Barney Kessler saw me, or thinks he saw me."

Meany spat. "Him? He's usually so full of booze he ain't never quite sure of what he does see, less'n it's another drink. Now, if that had been Van Lassen, he would have come right through that window glass after you."

"Have you seen him in town?"

"Every day, just about. Beats me how he can loaf and drink most all day without working."

"I wonder," said Jim. He drained his cup.

"Usually shows up at the Grape Arbor as soon as Baldy Victor opens up at ten o'clock. Him, Barney Kessler, and Buck Grant."

Jim pulled on his pants and then his boots. "Al Hitchins saw me, but he's dead. Brady Short is still running."

"What about his missus?"

"She could have let him kill me. She doesn't care anything anymore about Brady. Right now she's playing the wine jug. She doesn't care about *anything*."

"All the same, you'd better stop playin' a lone hand. You ain't killed anyone yet, but you keep foolin' around and you will. Murray Cullin never accepted the fact you was cleared of killin' young Crowley. Best thing for you to do is go see him, explain everything, and let him settle this business. Cass Crowley was like a brother to him. Besides, Murray Cullin is the law in this county, and you know damned well he is. He won't sleep or eat until he rounds up Brady Short. He never had much use for Brady Short, anyways."

Jim nodded. He was tired. Mentally and physically he felt the great strain that had been on him this past year. Murray Cullin really had nothing on Jim except the fact that he still believed Jim was guilty of the killing of Curt Crowley, but he was still lawman enough to know he had to have definite proof, not just suspicions.

Jim washed out in the stable, shivering in the damp cold. Winter was closing in. He dressed slowly, fortified himself with another cup of coffee and then peered through the fogged window. The drifting mist was almost opaque, swirling slowly through the seemingly deserted streets. Now and then the sound of voices came to him, magnified by the fog. He left the stable by the rear door and walked softly to the street, right about where he had stood almost a year ago to witness the mob breaking into the jail. It was almost nine-thirty. He looked quickly up and down the street and then crossed it swiftly, angling toward the ugly, slab-sided two-story building where Murray Cullin held forth when he wasn't out on other business.

Jim stepped into the deep-set doorway and opened one of the two double doors, letting himself into the hallway that led past the sheriff's office to the bullpen and the cells. The place seemed empty of life. The narrow staircase that led up to the county offices was to his left. He peered up the staircase. There were no lights up there, and then he remembered that county employees worked only part time and never on Saturdays.

He looked back over his shoulder and then opened the door of the sheriff's office. The tall, broad-shouldered lawman was seated in front of the big stove, warming his hands. A coffeepot sat atop the stove with a wisp of steam coming from the spout. Murray Cullin turned his swivel chair slowly as Jim walked toward the desk. "Murdock," he said coldly. "Come to give yourself up?"

Jim shook his head. "I have information as to who actually killed Cass Crowley," he said.

"A likely story. Those three men who were lynched here last year did the job and you know it, Murdock."

"Not me. Will you listen to me, Cullin?"

"Why not? Sit down. When you're done we'll do a little more talking about *you.*"

Jim sat down across the desk from the lawman. "Three men were responsible for the murder of Crowley."

"I know that! The three that were strung up."

"No! None of those three men could possibly have murdered him. It's taken me almost a year to track down their kin. Cullin, you've got to believe me on that score."

"All right," said Cullen patiently. He dropped his hands from the desk and leaned back in his chair. "Shoot! What three men were responsible for killing Crowley?"

138

"I know of only two of them, Sheriff. Alfred Hitchins and Brady Short are two of them."

Cullin narrowed his eyes. "By God!" he said. "Have you been drinking? Are you out of your mind?"

"No. I can prove what I say."

"Al Hitchins was found dead of a heart attack in his office early this morning when his chief clerk came to work. Accusing a dead man of murder is an old dodge, Murdock. In any case, slandering the name of a godly man like Hitchins will get you nowhere. What's your game, Murdock?"

"I said I knew two of them," said Jim quietly. "The second man is Brady Short, and he's not dead, Cullin. He's running like a coyote."

Cullin smiled faintly. "Great," he said. "You come in here and tell me you know two of the three murderers of Cass Crowley. Then you name a man who is dead and can't answer for himself, and accuse another who doesn't happen to be around."

"The fact that Short is on the run should make you suspicious."

Cullin waved a hand. "Brady Short is on the move quite a bit."

"His wife can tell you that he admitted killing Crowley."

"A wife's testimony has no weight against her husband."

Jim began to feel uncomfortable. He should have known better. Cullin wouldn't give Jim an inch.

Cullin eyed Jim speculatively. "Just for a laugh," he said. "Tell me why men like Short and Hitchins would want to kill Cass Crowley?"

"Hitchins was into Cass for a large sum of money. Payment of that debt would have ruined Hitchins."

"Go on," said the sheriff. "What about Brady Short?"

Jim felt for the makings and began to roll a cigarette. He lighted it and eyed Cullin through the wreathing smoke. "Cass had turned against Short. Short knew he'd never get anywhere politically without the support of Crowley. It is as simple as that."

"You've given me two good reasons, in your opinion, why Hitchins and Short wanted to get rid of Cass Crowley. That leaves the third man. Who is he? Why should he want to kill Crowley?"

"He must have been the ringleader. Neither of those two men had the guts to think up a plan like that and carry it through. They must have been sure of their hand. So sure. . . . By God! Brady Short tried his damnedest to stop that lynching and he knew all along he'd never stop them, nor did he want them to stop. Al Hitchins did the same thing."

"And the third man?"

It was very quiet in the office. Not a sound came from the fog-shrouded streets or from anywhere in the big building. Jim looked into the cold, hard eyes of Murray Cullin. *Then he knew*. Where had Cullin been when he should have been protecting those three innocent men? Off on a wild chase to get a change of venue from the governor, while his deputy was dead drunk and unable to stop the mob.

"Well, Murdock?" said the sheriff softly, very softly.

"You!" said Jim. He took the cigarette from his lips.

Something double-clicked beneath the big desk. "I've got a six-gun pointed at the pit of your belly," said Cullin. "*Don't you move!*"

"I wasn't thinking of it," said Jim quietly. "But why you, Cullin? By God, you had me completely fooled!"

The lawman's eyes narrowed. "I've hated Cass Crowley's guts for years," he said thinly. "He married the girl I loved. He got me over a barrel years ago and I lost my ranch to him. He tried to compensate by getting me the sheriff's job in this county, and I did the best I could with it. You'll have to admit that, Murdock."

"Granted," said Jim.

Cullin leaned forward. "He began to needle me about the death of his son. He wanted the killer brought to justice. He wouldn't let up on me, Murdock! I was sure it was you. A lot of people were positive it was you until that damned brother of yours got you cleared. I began to hate Crowley as I never hated anyone before, and he knew it! It was only a matter of time before he changed from backing me at elections to someone else. He could make or break anyone in this county, and a lot of men in this state as well. I had to get rid of him!"

"So you rigged an arrest of those three drifters and brought them in. Why didn't you kill them then, Cullin? *Los muertos no hablan*."

"They didn't have a chance. I wasn't sure that I would be unsuspected. It was Brady Short who thought up the lynching deal. It was Al Hitchins who agreed to pay off Van Lassen and the boys. You've got to admit it worked."

"Almost," said Jim quietly.

Cullin laughed softly. "Almost? I can kill you here and now and cover up. Al Hitchins can't talk. I can find Brady Short and shut his mouth as well, one way or another, Murdock. One way or another. You see, I hold all the aces."

The coal fell in the stove. A wagon rattled by in the street. A dog barked in the distance.

Jim dropped his cigarette into the garboon and slowly rolled another. "I left a letter with a friend of mine," he said quietly. "In it I have written everything I know. There's enough evidence in that letter to fully incriminate Hitchins and Short, but not you, Cullin. However, by piecing things together, and making an official inquiry, I think the governor may soon learn who the third man was who was in on the deal."

"You're lying!"

"Am I? Did you think I was a big enough fool to come back to Ute Crossing with a price on my head? I knew the odds, Cullin."

Cullin sat there for a long time, and then slowly he raised his right hand and placed the cocked pistol on the desk. "I might have known," he said huskily.

Jim lighted the cigarette and eyed Cullin over the flare of the match. "Who rigged my brother's buggy for that last ride, Cullin?" he asked.

"I don't know."

Jim fanned out the match. "It would be the sort of dirty work Barney Kessler would do."

Cullin wet his dry lips. "It was him and Van Lassen. Barney filed the kingbolt. Van waited on this side of the bridge until he saw Ben come out of the drive and head for the bridge. Van timed it to ride onto the bridge at the same time Ben rode out on it. Van slammed his horse against the side of the buggy. I guess you know the rest."

Jim stood up and waited. Cullin stared at the cocked pistol on his desk. "Get out of here," he said, without raising his head. "I've got work to do."

Jim closed the door behind him. He was in the street when he heard the muffled sound of the shot from the sheriff's office. "Score three," he said.

He looked through the wreathing mist toward the Grape Arbor. Down the street the clock atop Al Hitchins' Ute Valley Mercantile Company began to strike the hour. "Next time I ever get in a mess like this," said Jim to himself, "I'll be damned sure I do write such a letter." The clock rang for the tenth time.

Jim unbuttoned his coat. He walked slowly across the street. A man was walking toward the Grape Arbor. The man stopped to light a cigar, and when he looked up he saw the lean, scarred face of a man he knew well. Too well. . . .

141

"Buck Grant," said Jim softly. "Where are your drinking amigos?"

"I don't know, Murdock."

"You're lying. Don't try to call out to them."

Buck slowly took the cigar from his mouth. "I had nothing to do with killing your brother," he said. He glanced sideways at the saloon and opened his mouth to yell a warning. The heavy barrel of a Colt slammed alongside his skull and dropped him on the boardwalk. Jim stepped over him, looked up and down the street, then sheathed the Colt. He pushed through the swinging door.

A man leaned on the bar watching Baldy Victor removing the cork from a fresh bottle of rye. Another man stood in front of the mechanical piano idly flipping a coin in the air as he eyed the selections. Baldy looked toward the door and his jaw sagged. Van Lassen turned slowly. "Barney!" he said over his shoulder. Barney turned as Jim walked toward Van Lassen. His eyes widened.

Baldy stepped back against the backbar and glanced nervously from side to side. "Oh, my God," he husked.

"Have you been drinking, Lassen?" asked Jim quietly.

"What the hell is it to you?"

"I want no advantages."

"I haven't had a drink yet, Murdock. I will when I'm through with you."

"You know why I'm here?"

"You don't have to write it out, Murdock."

Barney wet his loose lips. His face seemed to go in and out of focus. "I ain't done nothing, Jim," he said.

"Nothing but a little filing, eh, Barney?"

Van Lassen smiled thinly. "It was him that done it," he said.

"Who drove his horse against the side of the buggy?"

Van jumped sideways from the bar, clawing for his Colt. Jim gripped the brim of his hat with his left hand and scaled it at Van's flushed face. The gunman flinched. Jim jumped to one side and fired at Barney Kessler as the man fumbled for his Colt. The first slug caught Barney in the guts, dumping him forward. The second slug caught him in the top of the skull, and the third smashed into the piano. It tinkled erratically into life.

Van Lassen fired. The slug whipped past Jim's face and shattered the backbar mirror, cascading shards of glass down on Baldy Victor, flat on his face on the duckboards. Jim fired once, jumped to one side, and fired again. Van opened his mouth in squared fashion like a Greek tragic mask as the

142

two slugs thudded into his chest. He fell heavily and lay still beneath the wreathing gun smoke while the piano ground steadily away.

Jim picked up his hat and placed it on his head. Slowly and mechanically he opened the loading gate of his Colt and began to load the hot cylinder. He could hear men shouting and calling out in the foggy street.

Baldy's head showed above the bar. "My God," he said. "No more than three minutes by the clock!"

Jim looked at him. "Was it self-defense, Baldy?"

"Absolutely! I'll swear to that!"

"They were your friends, Baldy."

Baldy brushed broken glass from the bar. "Hellsfire," he said. "They drove away more business than they brought."

Jim walked to the door and out into the foggy street. No one stopped him. He walked to the livery stable. He asked Meany Gillis to go to the general store on an errand for him. When Meany got back with the purchases, Jim had saddled the roan. He shook hands with Meany. "If the law wants me," he said, "you can tell them where to find me."

He mounted and rode east on the wide street. The wind was rising and the fog was being driven away. In a matter of minutes the wind had begun to hone a bitter edge to itself. It drove up the valley of the Ute, thrashing the trees and whipping the fog to tatters and then into nothingness.

Jim rode up the gallows hill. He dismounted and took a spade from the cantle. Slowly and deliberately he dug a hole at the base of the first of the three great trees that stood there. By the time he had dug a hole at the base of each of the trees the wind had cleared the valley of fog. People down in the streets of Ute Crossing could see him moving about on the gaunt hill.

He placed a can of Kepauno Giant Blasting Powder in each of the holes and carefully fused each one of them, then tamped in the earth. He lighted a short six, sucked it into life, and touched its end to each of the fuses. Then he mounted the dun. He was almost at the bottom of the hill when the first explosion came, followed rapidly by the others. Clods and dirt flew through the air, and the harsh echoes slammed back and forth between the valley walls and were lost in the windy distance. The trees thudded heavily to the wet ground.

He had a long ride to the west through bitter weather, but he'd make Three Forks before the passes were closed. He would be there in the spring if the law came looking for him.

He had a feeling it never would. As far as Jim Murdock was concerned he'd never ride east of Warrior Peak again.

It was almost time for the first snow of the year. There was a different feeling in the wind. A driving gust of it struck Jim's face like stinging, sharp-edged grit, and it wasn't until he reached the bottom of the slope that he realized that it wasn't grit at all, but the harsh reality of the first snowfall of the year.